Because it was you

Robert John Goddard

Acknowledgements

Having an idea for a novel and turning it into a cover picture design is hard. I want to thank Andrea for creating a wonderful cover for *Because it was you.*

andrea.price.concept

1

27 August 1939 – on the train to Verona

One of Tommy Mostyn's earliest memories was lying in the dentist's chair, wanting to be somewhere else and looking through a large window to find it. This feeling of misplacement, the desire to travel, perhaps in the hope of finding a better place just over the horizon, never really left him. Fifteen years later, he was on a train, relishing his future prospects and staring through the window at the roofs red and tiled, at chimneypots, cypress trees and cows from a barn being loaded on to trucks.

Destined for the knacker's yard, Tommy thought. *Just like Europe itself.*

And life and death moved on. The crimson and white leaves in the fields, the glimpses of towns both walled and towered, of markets with canvass and scent, all gone in an instant with the blow of a whistle and a shrill goodbye. So, what was next? The future beckoned.

What was next, perhaps, was brewing in the bay of seats diagonally opposite and neither window-watching life's possibilities nor *The Rubaiyat of Omar Khayyam* could distract Tommy from it. "It" was a man's hissing whisper and it was dragging Tommy into an ugly now of darkness, of shaded eyes, of an eye-to-mouth scar, hair greased backwards and the tell-tale black shirt and tie of the National Fascist Party.

Tommy glanced through the window, and the urge to break out of his confines consumed him, and he longed to tread upon the virgin snow that covered the faraway peaks, to keep walking beyond the horizon and sit under the portico of some pink, marble glory and, with his notebook on his knee, note down what he saw - the girls with ribbons in their hair, the men with a fedora, a trilby or a boater waltzing around them and begging favours.

"*Ebrea.*"

The word blazed across the train corridor, shattered both Tommy's dream and any illusion of just a domestic row, and it was spat out in the manner of something filthy and in stark contrast to the dance of vowels and consonants accompanying the rhythms and gestures that emerged from the other passengers in the train compartment. Tommy understood little of the Italian language but two and two together told him that the word "*ebrea*" meant "Jew," the word had been thrown at the man's female companion and Tommy knew the meaning of menace when he felt it and recognised a threatening tone when he heard one.

Tommy's eyes flickered towards the object of the man's disdain and his gaze lifted over his book's cover and settled on the woman's profile - a hat flopping over head and neck, sleeves of a jacket billowing over the wrists, and seamed and dark stockings stretched across ankles protruding into the corridor and lying one upon the other. Through the window, beyond the hat and the airy sleeves, other beauties struck Tommy, the early autumn turnings, from green to gold and from green to the red that wrapped around ancient walls and buildings.

When the man's whisper became a hiss, Tommy placed *The Rubaiyat of Omar Khayyam* on the table top and leaned forward, his weight over his thighs. The man's eyebrows were drawn together, but even though his waving hands poked ever nearer to the woman's face, her shoes remained one upon the other and, above them, her folded hands lay on the arm rest while her body twisted towards the window and her head tilted to one side, its eyes returning the man's stare. Briefly, she turned her head into the aisle and Tommy glimpsed her hair falling in wavelets over her ears, the alabaster of her skin and the big eyes and, through the window and into the landscape, his eyes caught the castle, fantastic in the autumn and surrounded by trees. And the feeling came to him that it was not she, but he, who was being threatened, he, who was being tested, his masculinity and his fearlessness challenged.

There was a muffled roar and the man's hand gripped at the lapel of her jackets. Tommy was on his feet, side-stepping into the corridor and a blur of open mouths and turned heads. He stepped towards the bay opposite. The man in black looked up.

"Stop this at once," Tommy said. "Leave this woman alone."

Tommy glanced sideways, caught her eye, wondered whether he was somehow related to the woman and why he felt both grounded and in a danger zone. The train lurched sideways, Tommy lost his balance, there was pain in his jaw, his vision went black and he fell backwards, hit the seat and began a slide to the floor. He shook his head and blinked. The man who had hit him was on his feet and tripping over the woman's outstretched legs. He toppled forward and Tommy grabbed his chance. He caught the man flush on the chin and he careered backwards, sprawled against the side of the compartment and fell into his seat, his hand brushing the ashtray and sending butt-ends flying. He spat loudly, glared at Tommy and slipped his hand inside his black jacket. Tommy was watching the fumbling hand, wondering what the man might be hiding under his arm when there was a sound from the end of the carriage.

"*Biglietti, per favore. Biglietti, per favore.*"

Ticket collectors were holding out their hands and demanding to see travel tickets. Their leg movements suggested restless urgency but they dragged their heels, looking into each bay of seats and glancing into the faces of each passenger.

The train was nearing the town of *Desenzano* and the Fascist slid his hand from inside his jacket and pushed himself to his feet. Brushing fag ash from his tunic, he stepped forward and pushed his face and its raised and pink scar so close that Tommy could smell the man's putrid breath. His eyes were still, but he used his head to turn them like a camera lens over every inch of skin on Tommy's face. He licked his lips, nodded to himself and his right arm rose, the hand held up in a sign of greeting. Tommy thought he was going to wipe away the trickle of blood that was running down from the corner of his lip to his chin. Instead, Tommy felt tugs at his shirt collar. The Fascist nodded and made a grunt of satisfaction.

"I remember you," he said.

Maintaining eye contact, he twisted his head sideways and thrust his chin forward in the manner of a man about to draw a razor across his chin. He raised his hand and tapped Tommy on the cheek.

"Sonofabitch, I find you," he said again, "*prima o poi* I find you."

With a nod of his head, he raised the index finger of his left hand, drew it across his chest and pushed the tip of his fingernail into the skin of his neck. Then, he drew the finger across throat to the other ear. A raised eyebrow, a questioning stare and he turned away, walked the gauntlet of eyes that would not see, that had already forgotten.

"Why did you do that?"

She was standing now and leaning in his direction and hurling words into his face.

"Why you do that? Who you think you are, Douglas Fairbanks?"

"Are you…?"

"Fine? Of course, I'm fine. The man is an old friend. He's harmless."

Tommy rubbed at his chin.

"He doesn't feel so harmless to me," he said.

"I not need no American…"

"Hero? I'm not American."

She shook her head and steepled her fingers.

"I don't need you," she said. "Just go."

"But…"

She tutted, and rolled her eyes.

"Just…"

"Ok, Ok, I'll go," he said.

She took his outstretched hand in hers and shook it before turning away. A last glance at the clinging skirt, the drooping hat, the billowing sleeves and he fingered the cut on his mouth and started off down the corridor towards the toilet noting the passing villas and facades in the first window, columns rising in the second and, in the third, the local people strolling and fretting in the streets, girls eating ice-creams on corners throwing glances at boys on the side-lines busy gesturing, talking and slicking back their hair. Tommy imagined he heard the entire exchange. It was an exotic hum of something different.

The train was stationary at *Desenzano* station when he returned to his seat. The bay opposite was empty. The girl had gone. Tommy felt not really there as if a part of him had gone away with her and the light was now a dirty yellow, like moonlight gone bad.

Picking up his book, Tommy saw that a piece of paper had been inserted between the pages. At first, he thought the conductor must have put it there. But he blinked when he saw the telephone number and his heartbeat quickened when he read the note inviting him to use it. At the bottom was a name, the uneven letters betraying the capricious movement of the train. The name was Carla and it signalled the end of a note from the girl with big brown eyes. This apparently independent woman had written this daring note, and Tommy, condemned to decipher it, did not try to understand the person who had written it. And when he got off the train at Verona, it was her face that dominated his thoughts and the touch of her hand that remained a firm and strong memory in the palm of his.

2

27-30 August 1939 - Verona, Italy

H otel Arena, signore? *Va bene*."
With the suggestion of a nod, the taxi-driver let
his sunglasses drop from his hairline to the bridge of his
nose and he squeezed the horn, fondled the gear stick,
pulled away from the station and, with much honking,
braking, angry glances, scattering of carts and middle-of-
the-road talkers, he drove towards the historical town
centre with so much speed that nothing remained still
and Tommy was surrounded by so much light that he
donned his sunglasses in order to watch the sun's rays
lighten the shadows under the porticos and turn every
doorway and wall into elegance and magic.

When they pulled up outside a Roman gateway,
Tommy shook his head.

"Hotel Arena?"

The driver pointed at a tall building squeezed
between the Roman gateways and the offices of
Regional Administration. He shrugged and said:

"Is in the little road there, signore, the *entrata*."

He pointed at a gap between the gateway and the administration offices and Tommy walked towards it with his luggage coming up behind him. He rang the bell at reception and waited a little but when nobody came, he leaned sideways and peered down the corridor. He was expecting a figure to appear from some doorway but the proprietor emerged instead from a recess behind the reception desk. The man's eyes stared out at the world through a bush of facial hair and a walrus moustache. He outlined the rules and regulations and then, without prompting, he gave a slow and huge shrug and said:

"And if you follow the rules, you will visit all the historical sites in our city, the Arena, the Roman theatre and perhaps, even Juliet's house. Yes, you can, if you want, do this."

Tommy said nothing, unsure whether or not the man was expecting him to respond. Fortunately, the proprietor continued with:

"But if you want to feel our city, to experience our city, to love our city, you must understand that history, however terrible, is always visible and developing in front of your eyes, Mr Mostyn. *Ha capito?"*

Tommy nodded his understanding, the proprietor winked and added:

"So – just jump in, be careful and enjoy."

He said nothing more - not a word about the museums and other tourist sites - and he handed Tommy his key.

Tommy rushed up the windowless staircase in half darkness. He supposed it was darker for those, like him, who had come in from the street. The presence of other hotel guests was signalled by the glow of a burning cigarette or a brush at his elbow and these encounters unsettled him in the same way that sounds from behind unsettled him while walking down a deserted road in the middle of the night.

He unpacked with every intention of going out, following his instructions and feeling the developing city but his determination was overshadowed by the piece of paper in his pocket, the telephone number and the invitation to use it. It presented him with the conflicting demands of his upbringing and his own curiosity. Upbringing told him that such an invitation was preposterous and suggestive of a woman with loose morals. On the other hand, curiosity was necessary for him to develop both as a writer and as a man. Curiosity told him to make up his own mind.

"I love you dearly, father," Tommy muttered while hanging his trousers, "but if you want me to develop into an independent man, then you must leave me to my own devices."

The first two days he ignored both the proprietor's advice and the conflict between upbringing and curiosity and immersed himself in the city's history. Consequently, there was always an excuse not to sit down, find the telephone number and use it. On the first day, he carried the slip of paper through the city centre, to the Roman arena and the *Giardini Giusti* where he enjoyed this fine example of an Italian garden and its terraces before, later that afternoon, exploring the area between *Piazza delle Erbe* and *Ponte Pietra*. Apart from the unused telephone number, the only blot on the day was the band of children engaged in a war game in one of the smaller squares.

They used sticks for guns and they imitated the sound of gunfire with inventive use of mouth and throat. When they noticed the young foreign man standing alone, the children became silent and staring before creeping towards him. Tommy was alone in the square and the sunlight while the boys advanced. Several storeys above, old and lined faces withdrew from windows, and shutters slammed away the sunlight and the unfolding drama in the square below. A black-shirt patrol passed by, the boys scattered and Tommy was left alone on the old stones and among the shadows. He moved on towards the river.

In the evening, he fell in with a stream of people crossing the *Adige* before heading towards the Roman theatre. He allowed himself to be carried through narrow streets, black and white squares, bars and old men playing with colourful cards and absorbed in a game in which sudden passions arose and cards were brought down with a crash on the table top.

On the second day, he took the train back to *Desenzano*, idled through the piazzas, visited the archaeological museum and admired the view of the mountains and took an earlier-than-anticipated middle-of-the-afternoon train back to Verona where, in the evening, he sat at one of a multitude of tables skirting *Piazza Br*a and separating the bars and the shop-fronts from the fashionable passers-by who materialised every evening to stroll and to socialise before dinner.

Tommy slipped his hand into his pocket and played with the slip of paper while scrutinising the groups of young men whistling and gesturing at the young ladies preening and strutting from one end of the piazza to the other but instead of looking for a telephone, Tommy became absorbed in these choreographed games of hide-and-seek, the cat and the mouse. More mature adults were nursing glasses of beer or wine. In fact, people of all ages were there from the youngest babies in prams to the oldest members of society watching it all from the side-lines.

What all these people – young and old, male and female - had in common was elegance. Young men swaggered in double-breasted and wide-shouldered suits, and two-tone shoes clicked and clacked while hats and sunglasses tipped over eye and nose and young women with their waspish waists, jauntily angled hats over enigmatic and Garbo-like shaded faces, set off in Tommy a shiver of excitement.

There was a sound of shuffling feet from under the walls to his right. Four or five black-shirted men had clubbed together under the medieval city wall and were singing the Fascist anthem, "*Giovenezza*."

From that moment, men in black shirts were everywhere and Tommy watched them weaving through the crowds, searched their faces for scars raised and pink while they joined the singers at the medieval wall. Within a minute, there was a large group of black shirts, black cavalry trousers, black belts and black boots putting all their vigour into this song about the future and hope. They were an impressive presence – at the same time, chic and noisy and threatening.

On the third morning, Tommy decided that he had paid enough lip service to the demands of his upbringing, that his conscience was clear and it was now time to focus on the demands of curiosity and immerse himself in the living history of the city.

He emerged from his hotel with a spring in his step and set off down the fashionable *Via Mazzini,* clenching and unclenching his fist around the slip of paper and her telephone number. *Via Mazzini* was narrow and dark but, entering *Piazza Bra*, he moved into the sunlight. The sun warmed his shoulders while he wandered through the garden in the centre of the square and he stopped to listen to the birds singing in the trees and to gaze at the knots of elderly men who had gathered in the square and who were now merrily chatting and orchestrating their conversation with expansive gestures while children jumped and scurried around them. Occasionally, a mother cried:

"*Antonino-o-o, Antonino-o-o, vieni Antonino-o-o.*"

Tommy strolled across the square and the mothers' cries followed while he reached into his pockets for some change and bought a newspaper from a kiosk on the edge of the garden. Looking up for a lit *Moka* sign, Tommy noticed the morning spring-in-the-step of men in aprons outside the bars. They were washing and scrubbing, and droplets of water sparkled on the table tops in the sunlight, while coffee machines were hissing and cutlery was clanging and brooms were whishing over the wide pavements. The odour of fresh coffee and pastry drifted across the square and Tommy marched towards it, pocketing the piece of paper as he did so. A breeze was blowing down from the mountains and brushed his cheeks while he settled himself beside one of the tables and he gazed at the hillocks rising green above the church towers.

It started as a sharpness in the air and was easier to feel than to see. He heard the distant crunch-crunching of stamping feet and he saw the people turn their heads and frown towards *Via Mazzini* until the crunching filled the air and a large group in black marched into the *piazza,* about 50 men, arm in arm and in lines of five, and they crashed to a halt when they were adjacent to the Roman arena and stood, an intimidating presence, amongst the strolling mothers, the chatting old men and the choreographed games of the young men and women.

The black shirts raised their arms in the fascist salute and their officer shouted:

"A chi la vittoria?"

To which everyone in the square responded with the Fascist salute and the shout that victory belonged to them.

"A noi"

The black shirts then stamped across the square towards the barracks and life returned to normal. Mothers continued pushing prams, young men tipped their hats over their eyes, young women swayed and smiled and waiters continued to wait at tables, but the table where Tommy had been sitting was empty. In some corner of the city that day he guessed that men of curiosity were taking a beating, women of independence were being assaulted and Jews were being ridiculed because they were Jews. Tommy had experienced enough of patriotic singing and soldiers claiming victory before a war had started.

Instead, he had dashed away to make his call. Time was short. He and Carla arranged to meet the following evening.

3

31 August 1939 – Verona

Eventually, Tommy grinned and nodded at the bags with belt loops, the polo shirt and two-tone shoes but, although the jacket, with its wide shoulders, emphasised his shape, the prospect of a warm evening brought a tight-lipped expression of uncertainty to his face. He removed the jacket but shook his head at his reflection in the mirror and dismissed the discord between weather and clothes.

Who cares about the warmth, Tommy?

Slipping back into the jacket, he touched at his forehead and brushed his hair into place with a swipe of his hand. Grinning and winking at his mirror image, he spun his boater on one finger, considered it from every angle, admired the ribbon with its double bow in his old school's colours and slipped it onto his head before making for the door.

He trotted down the stairs, tossed his room key onto the reception desk, dashed through the door and swaggered along *Via Cappello* in the cooler air and fading light of early evening. Slipping his hands into the trouser pockets, he decided to saunter round *Piazza delle Erbe* to test the effect of his look on the young people sitting and chatting in the shade of umbrellas outside *Café Filippini*. He pulled the rim of his boater over one eye and balanced it with an amused smile and a raised eyebrow whenever he was looked or smiled at – which was often. Satisfied, he set off down fashionable *Via Mazzini*.

Old men and women, sitting in doorways, squinted at him while younger women chatted and gesticulated and their children bounced and played amongst them. Towards the end of the street, *Piazza Bra* appeared to him as a thread of light between the tops of the houses. A few steps further and he discerned a slice of the Roman Arena and, directly opposite, the sweep of umbrellas shading and colouring the *Liston* pavement as far as the medieval crenellations of the *Portoni della Bra*.

Carla had suggested that they meet behind the *Liston*.

"In the bar with the red curtains," she had said. "It goes by the name of the Communist Bar."

Tommy tingled from head to foot. The apparent failure of Capitalism had been fiercely debated during his school years. It was agreed by teachers and students alike that the search for alternatives, which dominated this formative time, was shaped by the shadow of the First World War, the cult of mourning, single parent families and rejection of militarism. The leading contenders to replace the old order were Fascism and Communism and Tommy was personally acquainted with a cast of recruits to Communism. These included a war hero's son, a doctor's daughter, the adopted child of a well-known imperialist and the children of a bishop. Here, on the continent of Europe, he felt connected to the politics of his time and one step closer to bringing the matter, at least for himself, to a conclusion.

He had not been expecting a hammer and sickle and posters of Lenin to announce the presence of the Communist Bar, but he was lightly disappointed to find a building whose lintels, roofs and doors were no different from the lintels, roofs and doors around it. He trotted up the steps and, pausing to remove the boater and touch at his hair, he pushed at the door and went in.

A tall thin man with a handlebar moustache, and an apron tied round his waist, was standing behind the bar. Most of the stools around it seemed to be occupied by pullovers, beards and berets accompanied by gestures both sweeping and abridged.

"Can I have a window seat?" Tommy said.

The man with the apron nodded and led him through a curtain and into a large room with cubicles around the walls. Tommy supposed this was a quiet area but it seemed secretive to him and this was reinforced by cold glances in his direction, whispers over glasses of wine or beer and an irritable cessation of conversation as he passed by. The other guests seemed to be a mixture of government employees, students, and market vendors, and some of them wore the red beret. One middle-aged man was on his feet and arguing in whispers with several younger men. The older man waved a stick at them and left the bar. When Tommy took a seat in a cubicle by a window, everyone stopped what they were doing and stared at him.

Tommy was used to being admired and he enjoyed the attention he was receiving from the guests in the bar until he saw that he was overdressed and there was nothing engaging or flirtatious in the faces of those who stared. Their looks were sullen and hostile, and Tommy felt he had disturbed the rhythm of their thought and the flow of ideas. Topics such as the economy, politics or the latest dance music needed space to grow and develop and he had somehow crushed them.

He turned away and looked around. Both the window frames and much of the interior had carved wooden fittings and there were other smaller rooms around him and separated from the first room by low archways and red curtains. At least here, the eyes of Lenin looked down and blessed those disciples whose attention span had been but temporarily rearranged by Tommy's arrival and he was pleased to hear conversation had resumed.

Outside, the daily *passeggiata* was coming to an end. The sun must have set without him noticing and it was almost dark outside. Tommy placed his boater beside him and watched the daily ritual in its death throes. Walking shoulder to shoulder and dressed in military-style black, a chain of about twenty youths were occupying the width of the *Liston* and dominating the entire pavement in a show of power and solidarity. Most of the other walkers chose to take the line of least resistance, to shuffle around them or walk in their shadow. Watching it all from the terraces and balconies and with mild contempt in their eyes, the old people sat in judgement, their eyes urging the strollers to take heed and follow the straight and narrow. There was no sign of Carla.

Tommy was listening to the clanging of bells from a nearby church tower, and the *Liston* was gleaming in the light of the street lamps when groups of youths stirred. Heads turned towards the city walls and the world became silent. A girl with big brown eyes was walking in the lamplight. Tall and slender with narrow hips and waist she seemed to float, lifted by airy shoulders and puffed sleeves, over the *Liston*. Her progress along the pavement was celebrated in smiles and gestures, in eyes that followed and glittered at every curve and every feature of the face. The nose fell straight down from the forehead but it was probably the pouting lips that fascinated the boys. For her part, she of the alabaster skin took it all with a sway of the hips while her eyes, deep set and dark, looked at the people and things around her as if they were objects to be memorised. Tommy was captivated by her face, by her look, by her clutch bag, flared and white, and by the way she pulled it towards her stomach and held it between her fingers.

Sometimes, she looked beyond this world and raised her eyes to the trees that rose from the centre of the square. Was she looking for the birds, now delighting in the evening light and celebrating it with a final song? And when the song was over, there was silence except for the city breathing and living in the rising of the moon and there was Carla and it seemed to him that he had known her forever and that he simply had not seen her for a while.

She was there in front of him, standing still, a statue at the curtain separating the bar area from the cubicles. A song was emanating from the radio behind the bar and, while he listened, he took in her covered decorative buttons, the gathering of her dress and the fake flower trimmings. The singer crooned:

"Forget me as a sad memory. Forget me without too much regret. You will still find a smile of love."

Her head was tilted back with a look of defiance in the brown eyes. She appeared to dare, to tease him and once the impression was made, it became part of the natural order of things. Then she was walking towards him with her arm outstretched.

4

31 August 1939 – Verona

Tommy wrapped his hand around hers but he dared not gaze into her eyes for fear of losing himself and when his palm slid away from hers and he felt the stroke of her fingertips, he allowed himself a glance at her dress, tight at the hips and revealing the shape of her legs. She and Tommy settled themselves and Tommy was pleased the music from the bar was loud enough to deter them from speaking. While she cupped her chin with her hands, Tommy crossed and uncrossed his legs and wondered where to put his hands. He could hardly breathe.

He let his eyes wander to her hair, parted in the middle and falling over her ears and, smothering a desire to reach out and touch the alabaster of her skin, he put his hands under his thighs and sat on them.

Tommy and Carla remained like this, looking at each other and waiting for the song to come to an end and while they waited, the world outside was fading away, full darkness was settling on the town, and the tops of the buildings were merging into the night when, at last, the crooner raised his voice to reach his final note. Carla's eyebrows rose with it and into the voiceless silence, she said:

"So, can you tell me why…"

"We are here?" Tommy said. "You mean why…"

"Us?" she said. "Exactly. Why are we here in this bar at this time?"

Tommy's chin dropped and he struggled to find a suitable response. Tommy, who had won the debating prize in his last year at school, was speechless. Tommy, who had filled 10 notebooks with ideas for novels, had nothing to say. Tommy, who had been raised to believe that light conversation and small talk should always precede topics of a more profound nature, was struck dumb.

"I speculate," she said. "Perhaps, is because we happened to be on the same train…"

"At the same time?" Tommy said.

Tommy waited and let his eyes discover every inch of her face. It was not as if strong and independent woman were unknown to him. In her youth, his mother had been labelled "unladylike" and "unnatural" due to her active support of the suffragette movement. But neither his mother nor Carla had anything of the bitter spinster in them and nor were they masculine, plain or unnatural in any way.

"Maybe, maybe," she said. "But most of all…," and here she paused. "…because it is you…"

"And because it is you," Tommy said.

Tommy managed to squeeze out something resembling a smile.

"You know it," she said. "But I knew you were English as soon as I saw you on the train."

She stressed every vowel and even placed them where they did not belong. Tommy was captivated by the flaws in her English but he was also regaining some composure and her presence was now fuelling his confidence and enabling him to breathe again.

"I expect the book…," he began but Tommy's mouth was so dry that his voice squeaked and faded to nothing.

"The book?" Carla said.

Tommy cleared his throat.

"Yes, *The Rubaiyat of Omar Khayyam*," he said. "It must have been the giveaway."

She lowered her hands to the table top, let the fingers of one hand rest on the back of the other, shook her head and looked him in the eye.

"Giveaway?"

"Yes," he said. "The book was in English. Perhaps you guessed…"

"'My friend,'" she quoted. "'Let's not think of tomorrow'…"

"'But let's enjoy this fleeting moment of life'," Tommy said.

"Exactly. And it made me think," she said. "That this man, a man who is reading such a classic, must be a writer himself."

Tommy's eyes stopped wandering and focused. How could this person he hardly knew have identified what he called his unconscious companions, those moods, impressions and memories that appeared from time to time and demanded recognition? How could she have noticed?

"Writing like that in *The Rubaiyat* must inspire people to write," he said.

Carla waved an impatient hand.

"It is not other people I am interested in," she said.

She offered him a smile and Tommy opened his mouth but did not know where to start. He longed to tell her about his inspiration, the topics and themes that would fill up his work and the direction his career would take. He somehow knew that she would understand the moods and thoughts and involuntary inner images inflicted on him and beyond his control.

"It is you I want to hear about," she said.

He had thought long and hard about all the things that were important to him but till now, his dreams had fallen on deaf ears and his themes had toppled into empty spaces. Several agents and publishers had made a show of listening. Others had even asked to see samples of his writing but he had never heard back from them. His father had mocked the idea. His mother, practical and sensible as ever, suggested that he might like to go to America, get a job and start a family while he had a chance, while Britain was still at peace.

He barely heard the shout and clip-clop of feet running over the pavement outside when he said what he had never tried to say before.

"Yes, I want to capture the variety of ways in which the world can be beautiful, and to write them down so that they last forever and readers can enjoy them."

He studied her face, looking for a quiver, ripple or twitch that might betray her reaction to these words. He had been surprised to hear them himself because what he said had been unprepared, but it was her presence that had given him clarity and confidence to speak spontaneously and to articulate his ideas for the first time.

"And to do that," she said, "you will need the power of observation and creativity…"

"And judgement," Tommy added.

"And not to forget sensitivity and imagination."

Tommy pretended to imagine. It gave him the excuse he needed to stare at her. The truth was that he could neither take his eyes off her nor stop listening to her. He had never known how rhythmic language could be. Her words danced from her mouth resonant and clear and they inspired him, no – she inspired him, made him restless and eager to reach out, grab a pen or pencil and begin writing.

For a while, neither of them spoke, and the silence between them was not a silence of something missing, the awkward sullen silence of words' absence but the silence of content, the silence of just being there.

"And I want to be photographer," she said. "I want to capture the truth of the world and make to show how bad it can sometimes be."

Tommy nodded.

"Without pictures," he said, "nobody believes you."

"And memory is selective and short," she added. "But with a photo, you capture a moment in time and it lasts forever."

"A documentary then," Tommy said, "evidence for the future."

"Exactly, and…"

There was a commotion from outside. Something heavy had struck something metallic and the ensuing crash interrupted her. Turning his head to the window, Tommy peered out and tried to make sense of what he saw. It seemed that a large group of black shirts, some of whom carried flaming torches, had rolled a car over and pushed it onto the *Liston* and they were now circled around it, shouting and shaking their fists in the firelight while a brick arched through the air and landed with a crash on the petrol tank and other bricks followed and some men appeared carrying metal rods and axes while others were heaving a motor bike into the square.

"Look," Carla said, nodding to the torches, the axes and the violence. "You cannot trust the memories of the witnesses. The day after the event…"

"Yes," Tommy said. "The day after the event, everyone will tell you something different. And then they will take ownership of these memories and hate anyone who comes along and takes them away."

"So, you see," she said, "the only true evidence the future will have is the picture. The camera does not lie."

Carla opened her bag and drew out a small black object. Tommy was not surprised to see cameras in Verona. But their subjects were usually Juliet's balcony, the Roman arena or the bridges over the *Adige*. Carla viewed and clicked at the black uniforms, the hate, the energy and civilians imploring with gestures that suggested both sorrow and fear and she turned her lens to axes glinting in the lamplight, to axes striking and smashing both car and bike until, eventually, the evening walkers rushed to get away and, with the street echoing to the sound of metallic hammering and glass shattering, the ordinary people fled.

She put the camera back into her bag and looked through the window. The men in black were throwing up barriers across the entrances to the square.

"They are preventing people from getting in and out of the square," she said. "We need to go now."

She took his hand and he stumbled behind her towards the bar area where they passed faces both concerned and confused, and they half-ran into the corridor that led past the end of the bar and, leaving a vapour trail of alarm behind them, they raced towards a door on their right. Tommy slammed his shoulder into the door, twisting the door knob as he did so. But there had been no need for force. The door opened into another room. They stood for a moment in the doorframe and, glancing back into the bar, Tommy watched customers rising from their seats and moving in slow motion, staring towards the main door while they fumbled at the table top for any personal possessions – a hat, a scarf or a packet of cigarettes. One man made the sign of the cross.

He heard her camera clicking again. Half-concealed behind the open door, Carla focused it on two men who had pushed the entrance door open and stridden in. Both were wearing the woollen tunics of officers in the Fascist party. One of the men was tall and overweight. He lifted his head, scanned the bar and turned to nod at his companion. This second man was stockier than the first and both wore the Fascist black cap pulled down to the eyes in partial concealment of their faces. Before long two other men emerged from behind the bar. One was the man with the handlebar moustache and the apron who had shown Tommy to his table. The other man wore a suit. They stood in front of the two intruders and shouted at them and indicated with expansive arm movements that they should leave.

The shorter Fascist reached into his trouser pocket and pulled out a small pistol. Pushing the pistol against the barman's ribs, he squeezed the trigger. There was a bang, and the barman was flying backwards, crashing against the bar, sliding to a sitting position before toppling to the floor. Tommy froze. The assassin's black tunic was smothered in blood and smoke from the barrel of his gun was spiralling upwards and mingling with the tobacco smoke hanging over the bar.

The taller man then reached for a sheath hanging on the belt of his jacket. His hand appeared and it was holding a long and narrow blade. He raised his arm and brought it down hard towards the suited man's chest, but with a manoeuvre that Tommy had always associated with conjuring tricks, he reversed the direction of the blade and pushed the knife into the man's neck. The blade slid in without resistance. The man's eyes opened wide in response. There was a gurgling from his throat and his hands swirled as they reached for the blade. The assassin then stepped forward and pushed his weight into the knife, which sank up to the hilt. Tommy's eyes opened wide in horror as he watched the tip of the blade emerge from the man's mouth. He fell backwards and squirmed to the floor and the assassin stamped his foot on the twitching man's chest and, extracted the blade and wiped it on the dying man's jacket. The victim fumbled at his neck but the fumblings grew random, the fountains of blood grew weaker and the man fell backwards onto the body of his aproned comrade.

Tommy felt detached, not quite there, while his body reacted to danger. He heard the sound of racing footsteps. There was a crash of glass from the door area. Running feet were coming up the steps and in their direction. He glanced back into the bar area. The tall Fascist was replacing the blade in its sheath when he looked up, caught Tommy's eye, and froze. The light caught the lower half of his face, the raised slash starting from the corner of the mouth and ending under the eye and the eye rolled upwards and the man's top lip lifted in a sneer.

Tommy grabbed at Carla's arm and they both crouched and ran from the doorway. Tommy kicked at another door. The lock broke and the door swung open into a narrow courtyard. Carla appeared in his peripheral vision.

"He saw me," Tommy said.

"Who saw you?"

"The man from the train."

"Here," she said. "This way leads into the main street."

Tommy saw little. Carla was running in front of him. He heard screams from the piazza. He heard shots. He then grabbed for her hand and ran through the courtyard towards the streets. He glimpsed snapshots of violence. Angry words were exchanged. Angry words and the kick of an answer from a thug in a black shirt. Another man stumbled. A booted leg followed. The man fell. There was a shot. There was another shot. A man was clubbed. A woman was dragged away. And all of this to the delicate sounds of tinkling glass.

Then, the streets were deserted. The sound of their running footsteps echoed and bounced from wall to wall while they raced from facade to courtyard and skirted the edges of houses, dark doorways and *Madonnas* in walls and they careered through squares open and wide, bolted over the pavement of marble shining in lamplight, and they raced between the columns of palace and cloister.

Breathless, they emerged by the river. Shelter was visible as a glow of neon lights decorating a doorway with the greeting, "Hotel Arena" but the letter "A" was leaning sideways and flickering its way to an early death. Tommy held on to her hand and they walked beside the tumbling *Adige* in the light of the moon and tried to make sense of what they had seen.

"Did he recognise you?" Carla said.

Tommy shrugged his shoulders and shook his head.

"I don't know," he said. "Maybe."

"Then," she said, "maybe tomorrow he come and look for you."

Tommy pushed at the door of his hotel and the two of them climbed the stairs to his room. Carla said:

"But tonight," she said, "I am going to sleep in your bed. You will sleep on the floor."

"And tomorrow?"

"Didn't you see Scarlett O'Hara in *Gone with the Wind*? Tomorrow is another day."

5

1 September 1939 – Verona

Luca is still a bit in love with me," Carla said.

The words "love" and "still" hit Tommy like the crack of a starting pistol and triggered a series of images and responses: Carla surrounded by suitors, Carla as temptress, Carla in the arms of another man.

"Luca?"

"The poor boy you encountered on the train," Carla said.

Tommy fingered at the corner of his mouth before saying:

"Poor boy? You know him?"

"Of course, I know him."

They were breakfasting on the hotel terrace, at one with the sunlight and tuned in to the intermittent peeling of church bells, the sounds of a waking city, the aroma of brewing coffee and warm toast and honey.

"When we were children, Luca was the simple boy next door, the youngest of 6 children whose father had been killed on *Monte Pasubio* in the Great War."

The terrace breakfast tables were shaded by the colourful umbrellas that domed over them and their tablecloth picked up some colour from the Bougainvillea cascading down the side of the building.

"That boy murdered a man last night."

Carla raised her chin to look him in the eye and her knife fell with a clatter on the plate.

"Of course, it was murder, but he would not see it like that. Never forget what our generation of Italians learned at school. We children were the Fascists of the future. Boys had to be brave soldiers and girls had to provide Italy with the population. Mussolini was the only man who could lead Italy back to greatness. Luca joined his friends at after-school youth movements and they have all been prepared to fight for *il Duce* and Italy. In Mussolini, Luca found the father figure he has always wanted."

"Can't you make him see sense?"

Irritation tightened Carla's lips and pulled at the corners of her mouth.

"Must I spell it out for you? Luca has very little sense. The Fascist party uses people like him, gives them a feeling of importance. Luca now sees himself as a soldier who will help make Italy great again."

Tommy shook his head.

"That is no excuse for threatening you and for killing people?"

"Threatening me? He sees it as his duty to bring into line those who oppose Mussolini and his politics."

"You said he was a bit in love with you,"

"He is more than a bit in love with me. Unfortunately, the fact that I am a Jew is beyond his control."

"But not beyond understanding."

"No, but beyond the limits of his forgiveness and that means, in his world, I have betrayed him."

29

Tommy turned his head towards the river and watched its waters roaring and tumbling through the bridge arches and, just for a second, he thought he heard the river say, "Follow me, follow me…"

"Anyway," Carla said, spreading butter on a slice of toast, "we will need to keep a low profile for a while. It's very possible that Luca or his friend recognised us."

Tommy shook his head and said:

"His friend? The other killer, you mean?"

Carla nodded and kept her eyes on his while she turned her head at an angle, biting at the toast and wiping the corners of her mouth with her napkin. When she was ready, she added:

"And if they have seen the camera, we will be on their wanted list."

Tommy raised his hand and a waiter appeared at their table. While coffee was poured and the Bougainvillea admired its own glowing reflection in the terrace walls, Tommy let his mind touch on cameras and wanted lists, and then, forgot them. A light breeze brought with it a smell of flowers and Tommy enjoyed the air on his face, let it play around his ears, neck and nostrils and tease the lock of hair hanging over his forehead. Carla busied herself with peeling an apple and, without making eye contact, she said:

"The problem is, we are different from the others. If they see us, they remember us."

Carla is certainly different from any other woman I've known, even if the only other woman I've known well is my mother.

But his mother had been born in 1900 and was, in many respects, an Edwardian lady.

And so very different from the liberated, liberating, opinionated, challenging, independent and wonderful women sitting opposite me on this brilliant and beautiful blue morning.

Tommy smiled and dared to reach out to touch her hand with his fingertips.

"There are plenty of other men like me in Verona," he said.

Carla lifted her hand, waved her index finger from side to side and made a clicking noise with tongue and teeth.

"Not in the Communist Bar," she said.

"No, there is really nothing special…"

She snatched her hand away from his, raised her arms and let them hang in the air, tense and angular.

"No, Tommy. You don't understand, do you? Listen to me."

Seeing the disbelief and hurt on his face, she took a calming breath and placed her hand - spider-like - on his forearm.

"They are your clothes," she said.

"My clothes? They are no different from the clothes worn by Italians…"

"No, no, Tommy. You wear them like an Englishman," she said. "This and your behaviour make you…very special."

Tommy shook his head.

"*Un gentiluomo*," she said and she lowered her head and looked up and melted him with her big brown eyes. "Like a gentleman."

Tommy guessed what she was referring to. Neither of them had slept in the bed that night. They had dragged the sofa across to the open balcony doors to feel the cooling breeze. Fully dressed, with the memory of the killings they had witnessed and the shock that had followed, they sat in silence, hand in hand, and gazed at the city spreading out below them. And Tommy felt this experience binding them. Her hand was in his and, while they both thanked God for their lives, Tommy developed a strong sense of disappearing from other people's memories, that he was forgotten back home in England and the only life he had was here and now, on this balcony and with her hand in his and her head on his shoulder and in this beautiful city, a living and breathing city under the moonlight with voices whispering through the alleys, and doors springing open or closed in unseen apartment blocks and Carla burrowing for comfort in the warmth of his body, nestling her head on his shoulder and sleeping.

On several occasions, he stared at her profile, the straight nose and the pouting lips and, unable or unwilling to sleep, Tommy heard the striking of each hour from the city's many towers and he counted every clang, drifted with its echo across the rooftops and wished that time would stop so that he could follow that one sound across the city forever but, somewhere in his mind, he knew this time belonged to a dream and he knew it was a dream and he knew it would come to an end but he also knew it was a dream he would dream for the rest of his life.

Eventually, the night silence died away and over the expanse of roofs and church towers the sky began to lighten. When they appeared for breakfast later that morning, the hotel proprietor had taken the situation in his stride.

"A table for two? Certainly sir. Would sir and madam prefer to sit inside or out?"

"On the terrace, please," Tommy said. "And in the sun."

"Certainly, sir. And would sir and madam prefer coffee or tea?"

A white cuff and a waiter's hand reached into their world, replaced the old with the new and brushed the tablecloth. Carla smiled her thanks.

"Yes, an English gentleman," Carla said. "But you still don't understand, do you?"

Tommy shrugged his shoulders.

"You know," she said, "until last year, I was a student at the university in Padova. Until last year, my father was a law professor in Milan. Until last year, life was normal here in Verona."

From the street below, a stamping of boots announced the arrival of a Fascist patrol. Someone shouted: "*A chi la vittoria?*" There was a pause and the response: "*A noi.*"

Carla leaned forward, cupped her mouth with her hands and bracketed the words that emerged from it.

"And then," she said, "I was obliged to leave."

The stamping of Fascist boots was still audible but disappearing in the scamper of civilian shoes returning to click, clack and shuffle and crunch in the roads and alleyways around the hotel.

"Obliged?"

Carla sat half in and half out of the sunlight. Every now and then, she would turn her eyes to the large tracts of sky, blue and serene, and the birdsong that seemed to fill it.

"I am Jew," she said. "Have you not heard what is going on?"

Below them and in the wake of the patrol, brightly-coloured young people were now moving in circles through the streets as though the Fascist patrol had been an irrelevant interlude. Older women in black, clasping shawls to their chests, reappeared in the streets along with the carts loaded with cigarettes and tables loaded with bread and sugar.

"Since September last year," she said, "Jews have been banned from attending university. *Il Duce* stands together with his friend in Germany."

On the other side of the river, the tops of the houses were bathed in sunshine, and the walls were splashed with the colour of geraniums hanging from window boxes. The boxes dripped water to the pavement and, in the daylight, Tommy saw pools of slime glimmering in the shadows.

"My father and mother are left for the US. They are telling me to come to them before it is too late."

Tommy stared into her eyes. He felt like screaming.

Tommy - you have found this beautiful woman; and now you are going to lose her to the Americans and there is nothing you can do about it.

But he continued to smile at her because she made him want to smile and he was confident that his face remained pleasant to look at, that she would see a happy face with dimples somewhere around his mouth and eyes that grinned his personality to the world. All night long while she had slept with her head on his shoulder, he had dared to let his mind imagine a picture of the lives they might lead. Life would be as balanced as nature itself. In the morning and in the evening, they would walk over the hills and pluck olive and grape from the hillside. There was a line of such hills on the other side of the river *Adige* and the chapel on the highest of these was now so old that it seemed to grow naturally out of the ground like the cypress trees that surrounded it. Perhaps, they would sit in the shade of its walls before wandering back home, he to his room and his books, she to her darkroom.

The waiter came to brush the tablecloth, remove dirty crockery and offer more coffee. Both Tommy and Carla shook their heads.

You are going to lose her, Tommy, and all because she is a Jew.

He took a deep breath and put the question to her that he hardly dared to hear.

"And you," he said, "will you go to America, too?"

She looked to the floor and shook her head.

"Bad, bad things are happening here," she said. "We're no longer in control of our lives."

"So, what…"

"Am I going to do?"

Carla shook her head.

"Europe is on the edge of war. Everything is coming apart. We are on the point of catastrophe."

She doesn't know what to do… How can she know…? Will she stay? Oh, God, please let her stay.

Between one moment and another, the morning had changed for Tommy. He felt his heartbeat quicken, his lips become thin and his hands clench into fists. He hated these Fascists and the ordinary people who appeared unable to stop them. The sound of chattering from the streets and cafes below irritated him.

If these people are not careful, their world will come to an end and history will blame them for allowing it to happen.

She watched him while he reflected and they remained like that for some time while a busy morning buzz rose up from the streets around them.

"But," she said, thrusting out her chin, "something positive can come from all this and we are here to record it for the future. I have my camera..."

"…and I have my books."

A horse turned into the street below the terrace. The cart that followed it squeaked and crunched over the stones. A peel of bells, running over the roofs towards them was taken up by other bells so that for a minute, talking was impossible. Eventually, Carla said:

"And we are on the spot. We have our fingers on the…"

"Heartbeat? Yes, and we are here to record it."

"The seeds of change are here now. They are in front of our eyes even if we cannot see them. That is the job of the future historians to uncover. All I can do, a simple photographer, is give the historian evidence by capturing the moment with my pictures. And you can…"

"Do the same? I'm not sure…"

"Listen, and imagine," she said, with an excitement that abolished all his uncertainty.

"Imagine that someone had sketched the birth of Christ. They could not have known what the future held and what the baby would become."

Tommy lifted his head to the sky but he was at once enveloped in sunlight so strong that he was forced to close his eyes, do as he was told and imagine.

"And you," she said. "You are the writer who sees it all. You are the writer who interviews the three kings, the wise men, Joseph and Mary. Your books would never go out of print. You would be immortal."

"A nice dream," he said.

"It is not a dream," she said "It simply means you must be in the right place at the right time and we are…"

"Yes, we are, indeed. Then, perhaps, my writing will have an impact and make a difference, but…"

She turned her hands palms upwards and held them in front of her as if in prayer.

"Why are you waiting? History is around you. It is not in the walls of *Piazza Erbe* or *Piazza Bra*. It is not at Juliet's house or the *teatro romano*. It is here - now, and under our noses. You have to risk it, see it, write it."

Tommy stared at her, trying to tone down the excitement he knew must be in his expression. Fingering for a piece of paper and a pencil, he reflected that something had moved and he was unsure whether it was he or the world that had shifted on its axis. But it seemed to him that good ideas were no longer good, and bad ideas were no longer bad. He was free of constraint but he needed her to guide him and to help him find his way. Her mere presence was responsible for the lightness of being that had enveloped him, that helped him to breathe easily, that ensured all his senses were receptive, and he was still fingering for his notebook and pencil when he saw, in his peripheral vision, two figures in black appear at the reception desk.

The receptionist was looking back at them through the bush of facial hair. The two Fascists were full of the confidence born of certainty and their faces shone with will power. The receptionist was shaking his head and shrugging his shoulders and when the two Fascists had gone, he came over to their table and, with his eyes fixed on Tommy's face, he whispered in Carla's ear. Carla shook her head and her smile disappeared and she squeezed her eyes as if she could not bear to listen. When the receptionist had finished, he nodded at Tommy and disappeared into his recess behind the reception desk.

Carla swallowed and struggled to speak.

"Europe is on the edge," she said. "He tell us to go away for a few days until the crisis is over."

"What do…?"

"Pack your clothes," Carla said. "I will be back for you in one hour. We are going to hide in the mountains for a couple of days. Our new lives start now."

6

1 September 1939 – on the road to Giazza

Carla accelerated the Alfa out of a curve, and a cloud from the road rose and covered the car with dust. A group of women, bundles of black under the weight of washing sacks, shouted and gesticulated while the car zoomed past. Tommy imagined reports of this roaring beast dominating the rest-of-this-day's conversation for the women in the village. Chatter around stoves or kitchen sinks would start with the danger presented by these cars in general, continue with speculation about this particular car and is occupants and develop, through forests of flapping linen, into rumours of runaway lovers. Tommy reckoned they were around 12 miles from Verona but this was a world which was either standing still or moving backwards and ideal for those who wanted to hold back time.

"Mamma and papa used to have a house out here," Carla said.

"Used to have?"

Carla nodded.

"Until the Fascists took it, we spent every summer here."

Tommy saw Carla's torso lose its tension but she took a breath, accelerated on another curve and the car sped out of the village.

"But, you know," she said, "we have our lives and our chances," and she thumped the wheel with her palm to emphasis the plural nouns "lives" and "chances." "Photography, writing, surprises, successes and failures…"

"Yes, indeed," said Tommy. "They all lie in front of us."

She took both hands off the wheel and, shrugging at the same time, she held them at her ears.

"We cannot lose our time thinking of what could have been. That we can do when we are old."

Tommy nodded his agreement but he did not dare speculate about what might happen if she made a habit of removing her hands from the wheel. Nor had he wasted time considering what could have happened had they been apprehended by the Fascists the previous night. He glanced over his shoulder at the vast spaces and searched the daylight for tell-tale plumes of dust from a following vehicle but the horizon was clear and blue and the hills beside the road were carpeted in copper and gold and punctuated by farmhouses and terracotta tiled roofs, and behind them, the land rose to join the snow-capped mountains beyond. Tommy closed his eyes, raised his face to the wind and took a deep breath.

"What we saw…"

"In the Communist Bar?"

Tommy nodded and exhaled.

"I was very…"

"Me too," Carla said. "It was terrifying."

"And I just couldn't get my legs to…you know…"

"You were unable to move, yes I know what you mean."

Tommy turned to look at her.

Shall I tell her what I think? This shared experience of violence and death has bound us together. Shall I tell her or will she think I am being too forward? Can I risk it?

Tommy turned away, stared at the road and imagined himself as an old man telling and retelling this story to future generations, his and Carla's grandchildren perhaps, eager for the description of gruesome murder from a distant past and every time he told the story he would picture the person with whom the experience had been shared.

"You know," she said, glancing into the rear-view mirror, "whatever happens next, we will never forget what happened in the Communist Bar and that means you will never forget me and I will never forget you."

"So, that means we are immortal," Tommy said, grinning like a cat.

"As long as we both do live."

Tommy felt his grin enter its death throes – the puckering of skin around tight lips and the flick of the head that allowed the grin to die in peace.

You may be freed from mortality, old chap, but sooner rather than later, you will have to return to England.

And it was sorrow that flowed back into his face, sorrow that would return home with him and the only remedy for that was the passage of time.

But what if the passage of time does not help? Imagine, Tommy, what if you avoid conversations about love or Italy for fear of opening old wounds? It could be worse, I suppose...

He broke out into a cold sweat.

Horror of horrors, Tommy, suppose you do succeed in curing your grief? Will that mean you have lost all feelings for her?

"Perhaps nothing is immortal," Carla said, indicating the road in front of them. "Everything comes to an end one day. Where are the Roman soldiers who came this way? Where are the Venetians and where is Napoleon now? We need to look at the future."

The tarmac in front of them stretched out long and flat under a lazy dust cloud. It was hot and there was not a quiver of movement in the trees beside the road. The farmhouses and the hamlets and villages that straddled the road seemed uninhabited except for the odd shadow appearing for an instant in a window or doorway.

"In the end," Carla said, "these conquerors left their footprints but nothing has changed and all these people, with all their sound and fury, were here today and…"

"Gone tomorrow?"

Tommy closed his eyes, breathed deeply, felt the wind pulling at the roots of his hair, and realised that he was content to be where he was and that he did not need a horizon or a glass window to give him the thrill of wanting to be somewhere else.

There is no better place for me to be than this here and this now.

If he was at rest, his surroundings were in motion, and Tommy saw himself as an eternal traveller who was lucky enough to have found the right person to travel with.

"Tell me more about your people," he said.

"Later."

Yes, later was a good idea because on this day and at this hour, every house, every tree, every field and every passing piece of tarmac reminded him that he was now on his way to being a writer. There were snippets of stories, what-if scenarios and inspiration in almost everything he saw rushing past him and, at the same time, the movement brought him to himself and told him that he existed and that Carla was there beside him.

And you love the comfort of being alone with her, don't you, Tommy? And you love watching her eyes on the road ahead.

Near the town of San Martino, they pulled up at a garage. In a cloud of slow-settling dust, Tommy poured water into the radiator and watched Carla's long and slender legs as she took the opportunity to stretch them. In the garage owner's hut, innumerable objects from chocolates to kitchen equipment gave them the opportunity to browse and exclaim over this brand of tea canister or that type of strainer sieve. They later remarked on the dead faces of the women in black and the man in greasy overalls watching them with mistrust. These people would never know it, but they, too, became part of Carla and Tommy's history, part of their mythology.

The landscape changed when they turned into the *Val d'Illasi* and headed northwards. Carla hurtled over hills of olive and vine and sped under clear skies and high clouds along the valleys while the silhouettes of fortifications stood sentinel on the hilltops. Then came apple trees and historic towns and buildings, *Polizia, l'ospedale* and back again to the vineyards, the olive groves and the afternoon sun shining and bringing with it the fragrance of flowers and grasses. Suddenly, Carla pointed at something ahead of them.

"*Giazza* is in front of us and between the foothills and the peaks," she said. "And our hotel is in the principal square."

Instinctively, Tommy leaned forward and strained his eyes. Darker things were rising like waves in the distance and the waves became a brownish yellow until sunlight enveloped them and revealed crags, towers and crevices. *Giazza* was indeed waiting for them between plain and peak.

He turned to look at her face and her hair, its wavelets blowing backwards over her ears and forehead. She was relaxed but her dark eyes were even darker as they concentrated on the road ahead. Slowly, very slowly, she broke into a smile and her eyes flickered to his.

"Stop it," she said. "Stop looking at me like that. We need to arrive in *Giazza* in one piece, remember? And did I tell you? The old people here speak Italian but they talk amongst themselves in a dialect of medieval German."

Tommy grinned. If she told him that dragons existed in *Giazza* he would believe her. After all, mythical creatures and damsels in distress always lived in these places with ancient languages. He kept his eyes on her when they started up the long winding road towards *Giazza*. When the curves were tight, he marvelled at the way she rested her fingers on the wheel and when the drops were sheer, he admired her skin, her nose and the pouting lips and he daydreamed.

Will I ever summon up the courage to kiss them? Will she let me?

Turning to look down the valley and towards the plain, Tommy saw no tell-tale dust clouds rising over the road. Nonetheless, light on the distant and miniature fields and houses was flickering to darkness and the air was no longer the so-blue-and-so-light air of early morning. Tommy managed to convince himself, for a few seconds, that late afternoon light was never so clear and fresh as the clarity and light of the morning hours, but when those few seconds had ticked away, he took another look, a checking look, a putting-your-mind-at-rest look but what he thought he saw was a flash – a sunbeam reflecting on something shiny and metallic and reaching him on the hills.

That is a car, Tommy...and...

And they rounded a curve and roared into *Giazza's* main square, and the what-he-thought-he-saw disappeared from sight.

7

1 September 1939 – Giazza

The air was filled with the fragrance of flowers and
the mooing, hissing, clucking and grunting of
frightened farm animals. While Carla ran the gauntlet of
local eyes and dashed into the *Giazza* Hotel, Tommy
stood beside the car and turned his gaze upwards to the
sky. It was early-evening blue with passing white clouds
tinged with a reddish hue. The square itself was lined
with timber-framed and crooked houses cowering under
an enormous church, which threw long shadows of saint
and gargoyle across the square and the well in the
middle of it.

Tommy slipped his hands into his pockets, kicked a
stone in front of him, followed it down the road and
round the curve and kicked his heels where he could
stare into the valley. The sun was hanging low over the
treetops and casting its light over the stream tumbling
beside the road. He listened to the silence, the stillness
and the concern and disquiet in his belly. A motorised
vehicle would appear as a flash of sunlight or as a cloud

of rising dust but Tommy saw nothing as he retraced his steps and pretended to study the village architecture in general and the buildings in the square in particular. In one corner of the square, there was a sign beside an entrance: *Polizia di Stato.* Tommy hovered for a moment, casting his eyes around the square, feeling a tingling sensation and wondering whose eyes were focused on him and brushing his neck.

When he arrived at the entrance to the hotel, he paused in the doorway.

Still feeling insecure, Tommy? Or is something very wrong here?

Certainly, the hotel interior had an air of indecision about it, unsure as to whether it was a bar, a post-office, a restaurant, a grocery shop or even a hotel as the signage suggested. Carla was standing at the bar and conversing with an old lady frail enough to blow away in a breeze. The lady was wobbling on a walking stick while the fingers of one hand drummed on the counter by a coffee machine hissing and spitting like an angry goose. Beside it was a cash register with the carved brass plumage of some mythical flying creature. Carla looked up when Tommy approached and the old lady drifted across the room to deal with some customers at the far end of the room.

"Looks like we are the only guests," Carla said. "Lucky us…"

"Don't tell me," Tommy said.

And she didn't tell him. It was only when they were having an early dinner of pasta and beans at a table by the door that she mentioned this hotel had one room only and that there were no other hotels in the village. Tommy nodded, refusing to allow the idea of the police station to take root and distract him from the here and now with its crooked and unbalanced bodies, walking sticks and tetchiness sitting at the regulars' table in an alcove at the far end of the room. Their talking and shouting came in cycles of predictability through the cigarette smoke. A monologue and nods and whispers were followed by head shakes and shouts and fists coming down hard on the table top and, finally, there was a period of calm before the cycle started again.

After dinner, Carla took his hand and they wandered through the doorway and into the square, up close and personal with the intoxicating scent of the night. The village women had at last removed their aprons and, after a day of cutting and scraping, scouring and rubbing their way through piles of dirty washing, pegging out nappies or darning frayed garments, they had come to socialise, to discuss washing, nappies, marriages and children while their men played cards and drank and argued over the important events of the day. Several of these men were now outside and leaning against the hotel walls, whispering and smoking. Nobody had come to collect water. The well itself had long since fallen into disuse.

Eventually, the old lady with the stick came tapping out of the bar to join the gathering at the well. She was shaking her head and muttering, "*La guerra? ...perdita di tempo...perdita di tempo.*"

The other women listened and then took up these words like a religious chant. Tommy touched Carla's elbow and said:

"What's that they are saying?"

"*La Guerra* – war - is a "*perdita di tempo*" - a waste of time."

Carla was circulating amongst the old women. Tommy saw nods and whispers and hands touching and minds meeting and frowns and smiles, glances in his direction while he, in turn, allowed his eyes to wander towards the corner of the square and noted that there was still no sign of life in the official Police building there.

Carla was sitting amongst the villagers and she took up the pose of the listener while the women spoke and gestured with hand and face until, eventually, Carla pulled herself away from the withered hands that pulled her close. It was thrilling to see how easily they loved her.

Carla was in a reflective mood. She said the old ladies had narrated a vibrant and colourful story about love and they had told it in the local language and in a semi-poetic style of the ancient myths. "*Perdita di Tempo*," had translated for her. It was this myth which had caused the women to come together and the men to argue. The story concerned the recent discovery of a body embedded in the ice in a nearby valley. A party had been sent to investigate two days previously. They had chipped and chipped at the surface ice until a stillness had descended on them. Preserved for 23 years was the body of an Italian soldier. The rescuers guessed he had fallen into a crevasse in 1916/17 and was about to emerge, haunt briefly and then disintegrate in the air of the late thirties. They found a letter written to his girl back home in *Giazza*. It was a fragment of feeling, frozen for more than 23 years and lingering on the mountainside.

The argument they had witnessed earlier concerned the letter. The intended recipient of the missive was still alive and married with children. Should they give her the letter or not? She was, perhaps, content with her history and happy with her memories. One of the card players had suggested that the frozen body was her memory because memory preserved as well as ice. Another player argued that the letter should remain in the ice where it had been found. One man disagreed and argued that the letter had been written for her and that she would want to read it. Who did they think they were to keep it from her? Others disagreed and said that the letter was the ghost of someone's hopes and dreams and it belonged to the past and anyway, what right did they have to tamper with the woman's memory? The only topic they were able to agree on was that they would, of course, contact the next of kin.

When Carla shivered, Tommy took her elbow and led her into the hotel and the sound of the radio news. Most of the old men had dispersed and the interior had an atmosphere of closing down for the night. The evening news sounded with a blare of trumpets. Carla told him the news reader was reporting that the British were mobilising for war. There were also reports of trouble on the Polish-German border.

"It is starting," she said. "We have so little time."

Tommy opened his mouth to speak but Carla grabbed for his hands before he uttered a sound.

"Don't talk," she said. "Let us dance, while we have the chance."

She almost dragged him to an area that had been cleared of tables and chairs and where one other couple were shuffling around the floor to the crooning of a singer.

"Tango?" he said.

He did not understand much Italian but he heard the word "*scrivimi*" over and over and was wondering what it meant when he felt her hand on his waist and her leg resting on his. He had been told by his dance teacher at school that tango dancers danced to touch and to feel, to be held and to hold, and to dance out their desperation and their desire to the tango rhythm and to make it all look both easy and elegant.

"Tango," she said.

She felt for his hand and, leaning deep into each other, they allowed their thighs to touch and their knees to slide up in invitation. Tommy wanted to pinch himself. It was the beginning of September 1939, and he was simulating love-making in a public place with this special and beautiful woman. And, he was going to forget the police station and who might be in it and he was going to have these few minutes of intimate public passion with her, even if he was going to fall over her feet, trip and lose the rhythm. Slow…slow…quick-quick…slow… Tommy said to himself.

The night deepened. The lights went out but the music went on. She leaned into him, her hand playing with his back and she rested her head against his chest. She raised her eyes to his and said:

"The singer is telling her to write to him, he says, '*Scrivimi*'."

She paused as they held each other tight and span round.

"The man is singing, 'Write to me, don't never forget me and if you don't have nothing special to say, don't worry, I'll understand, for me it is enough to know that you are thinking of me even for a minute because I'll be satisfied even with a simple greeting. It takes little to feel closer. Just write to me.'"

She buried her head into his chest while the music played, the moon rose and they danced into the night, spinning in the corners, promenading past the chairs and tables, weaving their world into the dance and holding each other closer and closer, and tighter and tighter, dancing in the darkness until the music stopped.

8

2 September 1939 - Giazza to Passo Pertica

Tommy stepped through the doorway, stretched away the sleep from his arms and legs and strolled down the road into the full light of morning. The mist, filling the valley below him, was a harbinger of autumn and its beauty filled him with delight. The backs of the hills broke through the haze and floated under a cirrus-streaked blue. Making his way back to the square, he delighted in the red and yellow flowers nodding in the fields but the crags and buttresses beyond cared neither for the flowers nor the transience of hours or seasons. The peaks dominated both past and present and Tommy would not have been surprised to see trolls, imps and other fabulous creatures walking these hills or climbing the crags and conversing in the local language. There was sweetness around him, a sense of being alive, a tingling of the skin that made him marvel at the time before her. From where he was currently standing, that time was joyless.

The last time he had seen her, she had been wearing high-waisted trousers, a waisted shirt and a woollen cardigan and she had been stuffing two Swedish army rucksacks with provisions.

"We see us in the breakfast room," she had said.

Tommy hurried towards the hotel and banished thoughts of life without her by eyeing something equally unpleasant - the entrance to the police station in the corner of the square. A shiver ran from his chest to his stomach. The door was ajar.

Is he in there?

It was impossible to say. From his spot in the sunlight, Tommy only saw a door opening into a black hole.

Tommy neared the hotel and hesitated at the entrance while delighting in the freshness of the mountain air. At first, he did not recognise *Perdita di Tempo*. Gone was the frail old lady about to blow away in a breeze. She was now a revitalised woman flitting between the tables, her skirts hovering over the floorboards, attentive to her breakfast guests and moving in time to the music emanating from the radio. She had exchanged her dark clothes for lighter shawls and skirts and she had parted her hair in the middle and twisted it in a knot on her neck. She looked 20 years younger. Perhaps she was expecting a friend. Maybe, Tommy thought, she had fallen in love.

A few farmworkers were scattered around the room. Some were drinking wine. Others were drinking grappa with their coffee. Nobody was drunk and nobody was dancing but everybody seemed subdued. Their faces were turned towards the radio, waiting for the next news broadcast. The fact that German soldiers were invading Poland and that Great Britain was mobilising for war was reflected in the glum faces of all of them. Perhaps, Tommy thought, they were wondering whether their lives would end up like the lives of their fathers in the Great War, out of their control and heading for the local graveyard.

Carla was sitting sideways to him at a table in the middle of the room. She held her camera in one hand and was rubbing it with a cloth. Occasionally, she looked up and around her as though expecting someone to come but when Tommy stepped into the bar and walked towards her, she was ready with her camera and, as quick as a flash, she clicked and jumped to her feet.

"Walk around the room," she said. "Quick, don't talk, just walk."

Tommy responded by opening up his steps and turning them it into a kind of dance while Carla drifted closer to him, raising the camera to her eye, lowering it and losing herself in the moment while Tommy turned and swivelled, stretched out his moments and looked straight at her, winked and smiled into her concentrated state. And then, when he was inches away from her, these simple, beautiful moments came to an end and her strength seemed to wash out of her arms and she lowered the camera.

It was the light touch of Tommy's fingertips on her forearm that brought her back to the room. Her eyes were sparkling and there was a splash of red to her cheeks.

"You are looking guilty," he said.

"I am feeling part of what I frame in the viewfinder."

Tommy shook his head.

"Photography is a 2-way street," she said, "a connection between you and the subject."

"I don't understand."

Carla took a deep breath and replaced the camera in her bag.

"OK. The fact is," she said, "the news suggests that you may find yourself an enemy alien at any moment."

Tommy backed away from her matter-of-fact tone as if a wasp had buzzed his nose but when he saw her eyes brimming, it was only Carla's outstretched arm and the finger waving in front of her that prevented him from leaning forward and comforting her in his arms.

"No, don't say nothing," she said. "Have you never heard of the Pact of Steel? It commits both Italy and Germany to support the other if one becomes involved in a war."

"But…"

"But nothing," Carla said. "You are at the wrong place at the wrong time and that can mean internment."

Perdita di Tempo was standing over them. Unruffled by Carla's outburst, she placed a jug of coffee between them. Tommy doubted she spoke English but she seemed to understand everything – an expert, perhaps, in the meaning of body language, facial and vocal expression. She spoke in a monotone while she poured their coffee and then drifted away. Carla said:

"She says that *prima o poi…*"

"Prima o poi?"

"Yes, - sooner or later - Italy will join their Fascist ally, Hitler. It is only a matter of time."

"But not today," Tommy said, smiling in a way that, he knew, accentuated his dimples.

"No, today not," Carla said. "But perhaps the next week and then I come and find you in your internment camp."

"Every day," he said.

"And I take more pictures of you," she said, getting to her feet. "Give me 15 minutes now and I meet you here."

Tommy's head was spinning. Life was moving so fast that a day was now a minute in this fairy-tale land of theirs. He looked into his coffee cup and stirred the brown liquid hoping to find something that might help him – a horoscope, perhaps, or inspiration – but there was nothing but a few coffee grounds. Tommy got to his feet, strode towards the door and went out into the square. He wandered between light and shadow, from street to street and back into the square. A group of men had gathered near the well. Above their heads, a couple of Italian flags were hanging limp from a balcony. Tommy heard the rumble of their talk but when he approached, conversation stopped and some of them turned their backs on him as he passed under the flags and made his way back to the bar. A shadow, shifting in his peripheral vision, stopped him in his tracks and Tommy flicked his head towards the police station. He stood there, breathing hard for several seconds and stared.

Mountains out of mole hills, Tommy.

"Or shadow people out of shadows," he said to himself and he stepped into the hotel to find Carla ready and waiting. The two army rucksacks, filled with beer and sandwiches, courtesy of *Perdita di Tempo,* were propped up against a chair.

"OK?"

"Wonderful," he said.

Perdita di Tempo took them to the door and waved them off. There was a twinkle in her eye when she told them they would meet Signor Pelagatti in his mountain refuge.

"Please remember," translated Carla, "to give my compliments to him when you see him and tell him not to be late."

Tommy and Carla agreed to do as they were asked and set off across the square. They sauntered along tiny streets to a place where the houses thinned out and the metalled road faded into a gravel path running beside a stream while to left and right the land curved upwards and steepened into the mountain sides. Tilting his head back Tommy was able to discern their path, a clear white line occasionally drowning in a rush of scree and zig-zagging up and away to disappear far above them and beyond their eyesight where they would find Signor Pelagatti and the hut where they were to spend the night.

"So, now we know why," Carla said.

"Why what?"

"She seems so young today…"

"Because she's waiting for a friend.

"She looks…

"Twenty years younger, yes."

"Why they no marry?"

"Maybe it's…"

"Better for them like that. But are they in…?"

"In love? Of course, they are in love."

The track thinned and steepened and entered a wooded area where it lost itself in the pine needles, and their rustling footsteps merged into the silence of the trees while a stream rushed and tumbled beside them and, from time to time, dived underground only to emerge further down the mountain with a joyous rush and gurgle but soon the trees were behind them and the sun appeared from over the mountain to warm them and after around 3 hours of tripping, jumping and trudging upwards to the rhythm of their breathing and the beating of their hearts, they rested where the gravel path levelled out on a rocky plateau.

"My parents are born in Milan," she said, "but they sold the house there to pay for their travel to America."

The early afternoon was windless and still, and the furthest peaks merged seamless with the sky.

"I am so sorry," he said, "I had no idea this was going on."

"Don't be sorry," Carla said and told him that her parents had once been supporters of Mussolini. "At least until last year and then the racial laws restricted the civil rights of Jews, banned their books and stopped them from public office and higher education. And that won't finish there. In time, there will be more laws, Jews will lose their assets, stopped from travel and probably put in prison."

Tommy jumped up and stood in front of her.

"Come back with me to England," he said. "Why don't you? You will be safe there."

Carla avoided his eyes, got to her feet and busied herself with the straps of her rucksack.

"And finish in an internment camp?" she said. "I think not."

Tommy laid his hand on her arm.

"You know," he said. "maybe the light is playing tricks with my eyes."

Carla stared into his eyes and frowned.

"The mist and the light," Tommy said, "they form a kind of screen onto which I can project my mind – especially when it is engaged in wishful thinking."

"And what are you wishing for, Tommy?"

Now is the time, Tommy, she is waiting for you…kiss her now…

"I am wishing that I…"

"Yes?"

"That I could…"

"Write a book and get it published?"

"No, no…"

The flickering shadow of a bird hovering overhead seemed to catch Carla's eye. The bird was large, dark and menacing and, swooping up, down and around the nearby crags, the bird was alert to danger, protecting its young. Sometimes, it paused in mid-flight, hanging hunched and tense, before diving again towards Signor Pelegatti's hut, now visible and half-concealed in the rock face above.

"You are a writer, Tommy, and of course you want to be published."

"You are, and you will always be, my inspiration," he said to her back as she flitted away from rock to rock and between sunlight and shadow.

Tommy was still around 50 metres behind her when a black and white individual emerged from the hut. Whoever he was, this individual was in a hurry and revealed himself as a white-haired, sturdy man with black bowler, starched white collar, black jacket and trousers. This, tommy correctly assumed, was *Perdita di Tempo's* Signor Pelagatti and he was clearly anxious not to incur his lady's wrath by being late.

It also turned out that he was deaf in one ear, that he ran the hut alone, had a few goats, some chickens and a room in the attic for guests. He did not often go down to *Giazza* these days, he told them, but he had recently had a premonition of some great disaster in which millions would die. He knew Tommy and Carla were climbing up the mountain and had waited until catching sight of them before going down to join "his signora" in *Giazza* and to warn her. He had left some bread, cheese and other bits and pieces for them. The hut was never locked and they could sleep in the attic. He had to hurry away, he said, because she was expecting him to arrive on time and because rain was on the way and without a word more, he plunged downwards at a speed which belied his age. Tommy watched his bowler, the perfect fashion accessory that turned every man into a gentleman, zig-zagging down the mountainside.

Somewhere, rocks were falling and shadows were creeping down the buttresses and moving across the high alpine plateau to surround but not engulf a grassy hillock in shadow. This island of light in the late afternoon sun renewed Tommy's optimism.

"Perhaps," he said, "you should follow your parents and go to America."

"Maybe," Carla said. "Mussolini passed these racial laws to make his German friends happy. I do not say that there is widespread and real anti-Semitic behaviour here in Italy."

"Despite the killing we saw in Verona."

"That was probably the... how do you say, "*protezione*?"

"Protection racket?"

"Exactly."

They ate bread and sausage and drank beer, discussed *The Four Feathers* and *Gone with the Wind*, dissected Coco Chanel and Pablo Picasso and they talked and laughed until they forgot that the sun was now about to set, daylight was fading fast and an icy mantle of blue was spreading over the snow-covered mountains to the east, and far beneath them, and shrouded in a soft mist, was the forest they had passed through, now turning early-autumn brown and yellow and reaching out like tentacles and gripping the rocky buttresses rising from the valley floor to reach them on the hillock. Winding down the valley and trailing away into the trees was the path they had taken and beside it, the dying light glinting off its waters, the stream rushed and tumbled and plunged down to *Giazza*.

"Look there," Carla said.

She was pointing at the clouds which, for most of the day, had been tight and contained on the horizon but now, as though released from all restraint, they were billowing upwards and threatening to come down on them. This was the moment.

"We had better go to the hut..." Carla said.

Oh, God. This may be the time.

She brushed his hand with hers and, opening her mouth to say something, she said nothing.

Christ. What exactly will she be expecting?

Tentacles of clouds were rolling over the path and the crags steamed before their eyes and disappeared in the mist. Carla grabbed at Tommy's elbow, and there was that face, those eyes and that hair, just out of his reach while they stumbled down to Signor Pelagatti's hut.

The wind was gaining strength and Tommy peered into the gathering darkness and saw flickering, as evil as it was beautiful, deep in the clouds. A sudden gust, harsh and stinging, smacked raindrops at his cheeks and, reaching out for her, he pushed her inside and both of them fell towards the stairwell, their feet rubbing on the wooden step in this perfumed pitch-black of night. Carla was in front of him – a familiar shape from his dreams and she slipped past and fumbled at the fasteners of her outer garments and the wind moaned and lightning flashed, stringing lights around her that flickered butterflies on her skin. A crackle of static, the slide and rub of material charged him with feeling.

Oh, God – we're going to do it...

A howl of wind, the storm came closer and rain pelted the windows. A flash, flickers of light on her face and she shot out of the darkness and took his breath away. Those years of talking, bragging, speculation, masturbation and lying were about to come to nothing.

Oh, God, please help me do it now, please..."

He put out his arm to find and close the door but before his palm found the wood, Carla's hand fell into his and in a feeble sheet of lightning he saw her head turned expectantly towards his. Her breathing was heavier and there was a look in her eyes that suggested she had given consent to a request he had not made.

Now is the time.

She reached out and pulled him towards her. He shuddered, searched for her eyes in the darkness and felt himself changing. He wanted to speak, to tell her he was a just a boy, that this boy loved her and more than anything in the whole wide world, he wanted her to love him too. Instead, he cupped her face between his hands and everything slipped into place as he tilted her lips towards him.

9

3 September 1939 - Via delle Creste to Giazza

The sense that his life had changed strengthened, and Tommy climbed to the rhythm of his heart, his breathing and the clip, clipping of carabiner on the safety cable. Hugging the rock face, reaching for the next handhold, Tommy kicked piles of stones spraying downwards. He heard them gather pace and echo down the gulley in which he and Carla had been climbing.

Tommy emerged in an open and flat space, the safety cable ended and he unclicked his carabiners for the last time. Now breathless and above the tree line, he settled himself on a cracked and ancient boulder and, while waiting for Carla to join him, he peered over the gulley and down upon the browns and greens of the forest and merely noted that the green of the trees had faded, as colours will do towards summer's end, and that the treetops were swaying in a breeze.

Tommy breathed deeply, felt the air enter his lungs and fill him with life. He was bursting with joy and with freedom: joy because he was with the woman he most wanted to be with, and free because he was on the cusp of living his own life, making his own choices, getting involved and no longer looking at life through a glass window.

Out there, on the edge of a precipice, Tommy tensed.

Gripping at the safety harness, he leaned into the void, held his breath and scanned the forest. There was a flash of colour amongst the trees. A second later it was there again, a flash of blue, a waterproof jacket perhaps, and it was getting nearer. With an expulsion of breath, Tommy straightened up. He swayed for a moment as a gust of wind caught him off-balance but, clenching his fists, he leaned forward as if the wind were a force against his will and he was still standing like this on the mountain edge when Carla came, head bobbing, along the ledge to join him.

Tommy allowed his eyes to linger, as he often did, on her hair, its wavelets now blowing over her ears. He shook his head and wondered whether he was in fact living his own life and this time with her was just a dream, and he pinched his arm to assure himself that indeed it was true.

"Do you think they love each other?" Tommy asked.

"Who?"

"*Perdita di Tempo* and Signor Pelagatti."

"Perhaps, they love each other but cannot live together."

"Maybe, he needs his solitude."

"Maybe she needs hers," Carla said.

"They will never get married."

"Do they need to? Perhaps, by keeping a distance, they keep their love alive. And I want to show you something."

It was early morning. The clouds were covering the sky like an almost-fully-extended Venetian blind and sheets of sunlight were bursting through the cloud-slats.

She put her hand on his shoulder and, raising her other arm, she pointed into the distance.

"You see? That long mountain over there is *Monte Baldo.*"

There was a silence beside her. Tommy had made no pretence of following the direction of her finger. His eyes were roaming over her face but, realising that something was expected of him, his eyes sharpened and focused, and he said:

"Where Lake Garda is?"

"Yes, and behind *Monte Baldo* is Napoleon's Nose."

"Really?" Tommy said, admiring the curve of her nose.

"Legend has it that during the Napoleonic wars, French soldiers billeted in this region saw a similarity of the mountain silhouette to Napoleon in profile. Even today, the locals call this mountain, "*il naso di Napoleone.*"

In his peripheral vision, Tommy saw Carla's pointing finger. He said:

"You're wonderful."

The sky was ever clearer and the mountain tops on the furthest horizon were now pushing through the Venetian blind and floating above the earth. There were three peaks in particular, almost identical in size and shape, and each peak had one little feather-like cloud over its summit.

"They are making a show for us," Carla said. "They will whisper their stories to those who listen. Look there."

"Where?"

"There."

Nestling his head between her shoulder and neck, he looked along her outstretched arm.

"There" was a mountain called *Monte Pasubio* and it seemed to him that it was hanging on the end of Carla's pointing finger. Beyond it, the Veneto plain stretched out to the towns of Vicenza, Venice and the sea.

"These mountains have been doing this trick since the beginning of time," Carla said.

"Oh, yes."

"Yes, they give the impression that time is an illusion. Here, nothing changes. People walking on these hills centuries ago would have seen the same thing that we are seeing today."

Tommy remained silent for a while. Eventually, he said:

"Why us? And why this dangerous moment, this time of war and unrest?"

Carla spread her arms out wide and shook her head.

"Because it is…"

"Yes?"

"Because it is now. Because it is me and because it is you…"

They sat down together and watched a silver shaft of burning light in the distance towards Venice.

"It's the Adriatic Sea," Carla said. "It is the opportunity of a lifetime to see that from here."

A sensation like a mild electric shock passed from her body and into his and Tommy felt it as a warm glow tingling in his arms and in his heart.

"I will never forget this moment," she said.

She plucked an edelweiss plant from the sea around them and brought it to her lips and then held it out for him to take. He cupped her hand in his, drew the petals towards him and, as though it was the most fragile thing in the world, he brushed the flower with his lips. Then, she slipped it away in the top pocket of her blouse.

"Never, Tommy," she said. "Never will I forget this day, this flower, this time with you."

He glanced at her face and he never doubted her sincerity and nor did he doubt that his world began and ended in Carla's big brown eyes. He felt himself moving away from this moment and he sensed the person he would become and the path he would take. He was already taking mental notes, listening to his dreams, and his fingers closed as though around a pencil. Not only was he going to be a writer, everything he wrote would have its source in this time together with her above Giazza.

Looking towards the sky, he saw that it had momentarily disappeared behind an archway of clouds and below the arches, the trees were swaying to a quickening wind. Tommy refused to blink for fear of missing the ways in which his dreams were taking shape in front of him. He stared into the spaces between the trees and saw them as bottomless hollows in which this time with Carla and his future life existed side by side. He knew he would never forget Carla or Napoleon's nose, Venice, the flowers, *Monte Pasubio* and first love. And he knew that every word he would write, every space between them, every chapter, every paragraph, every sentence, every clause and phrase, every comma, every semi-colon – and he liked semi-colons - every full-stop and every header and footer would contain elements of her.

Fool, Tommy. Don't you know that this beginning is coming to an end? Prepare yourself for the new life. Let your memory inspire you.

About one hour later, they were in a gulley above the *Giazza* valley. There were shouts and echoes from in front of them. A quickening of movement and surprise at finding three men repairing the fixed safety ropes along the route of their climb. Tommy's world was in a whirl of red woollen socks, curved and powerful legs, knee breeches, the alpine hats with the raven feather, and Carla's eyes big and brown in the sunlight. There was an exchange of words, a tumbling of language and then the men were behind them.

She held out her hand and they made their way up the *Via delle Creste* to the summit hut where Tommy found friendliness, curiosity about his nationality, Carla's wavy hair and pouting lips, her alabaster skin, a group of schoolchildren singing mountain songs, Carla's brown eyes and the shouts for wine and food as the "maintenance men," bustling through the door, greeted the young lovers like old friends before Tommy and Carla were out of the door and setting off down the mountain.

They walked hand in hand below the summit peaks. From the meadows, they marvelled at the crests dropping like curtains to the valley. They jogged through a light wind and grasses fresh with life, busy with grasshoppers and edelweiss, ferns and wild blueberries. While they sailed through the afternoon, Carla named the prominent peaks on the horizon: *Cima Mosca*, *Bocchetta dei Fondi* and *Monte Obante*.

Tommy did not recognise the trenches, but often here and increasingly there, shreds of barbed wire pushed through the stones, and the rocks were splintered and sharp; somehow cleaner than the surrounding rocks, white against brown.

"Mines exploded here in 1916 and the bodies were never taken away."

"So, we two are walking on a graveyard," Tommy said. "What are we…"

He had already begun the drop to his haunches, begun the removal of weight from the knees, when he felt as though his head had made contact with a cricket bat swung with all the batter's energy. Pain blasted inwards from the point of contact. Bright flashes of light appeared like stars. There was no pain, but he could not move.

Is there blood? Have I lost any teeth? Is my nose broken? Where is she?

There was a numbness on the left side of his face. He lay on his back with a heavy and wriggling weight upon his chest. And the weight had a scar on its cheek, a smell, both rancid and stale and the skin was clammy, the black eyes fixed on him with a wicked gleam, cruel eyes of the kind that you never survived, that made you want to look away, and the man's tongue was appearing and disappearing, flickering and pulsating and licking his smiling lips.

Tommy wanted to scream but his voice had left him, his eyes were bursting and he was struggling to breathe with a clamp around his throat. Another shape appeared. There was thwack and the weight went limp.

For a moment Tommy realised that the person on top of him was not going to shift. With difficulty, he wriggled from beneath the great weight and, struggled to his feet and gazed down upon the man who had tried to hurt him. He saw the truncheon that had struck him and a wave of exultation swept over him.

"Tommy, Tommy…"

"He was just unlucky," Tommy said. "Caught me as I was about to crouch down."

Carla relaxed with bursts of laughter and sighs of relief.

"I am fine," he said over and over in response to Carla's questions and he noted the boulder she still held that had rendered Luca unconscious.

"There's no blood," he said.

"You must go to the hospital…"

"No, no…"

"Let them check you over."

"Believe me," Tommy said, "I'm fine.

"*Testardo*," she said. "Stubborn like a…"

"Mule?"

68

"No – like a man of the mountain."

"You saved my life," he said.

Carla dropped to one knee beside Luca, took out a coil of mountain rope from her rucksack and tied it around his ankles and wrists and pulled it tight. There was a stream of blood running down Luca's chin.

"Luca's jaw is broken," Carla said. "He will need hospital treatment but he won't bother us again today."

Tommy was rubbing at the crown of his head and scanning the upland, the forests below and the crags around them.

"Did he act alone?"

"He must have followed us yesterday," Carla said.

"But was he alone or…"

"Alone," Carla said. "Luca actually prefers to act alone."

"That's not what we saw in Verona."

"No," Carla said, "but this is a private matter and it is not over yet."

Tommy studied Luca's powerful body. The thought crossed his mind.

Kill him now while you have the chance. Kill him before he kills you.

Tommy shook his head and he hurried after Carla, through the deep clanging of nearby and far-off cow-bells. For Tommy, the sound carried a haunting quality, a reminder of death and that all things would soon come to an end. Scrambling down the scree slope to the refuge at *Passo Pertica*, Tommy noticed man-made caves, more trenches and metal crosses.

Tommy sensed someone behind him.

He was as sure of this presence as he was sure of his own existence. Spinning round, Tommy brought his guard up to protect his face but the figure was far away and taking shape as it neared. It was Signor Pelagatti. He was shaking his head, spoke in whispers to Carla and then passed them by with barely a nod of the head. She said:

"The war has started. Great Britain is at war with Italy's friend, Germany."

"Let's go this way," Tommy said, following a sign that took them through wooded slopes to the minor summit of *Cima Trappola.* The sun had been high in the sky when they set off from the hut but now the sun was about to go down and she came and nestled her head on his shoulder and used her free arm to rub around the lump that had grown on the crown of his head.

It was that time after noon when the light mellows and the mountains whisper to those who listen. The colours faded, as colours will in the light of dying day, until the furthest hill weighed low and darkly on the horizon. At this time of stillness, when the air of invisible things brushed the tips of the long grass, Tommy heard again a distant cry. From some place beyond the vanishing point a person had come and called out to him. The voice seemed familiar yet insistent - perhaps it was his own voice with a new tone and it was calling him towards his destiny.

"Hurry, Tommy, hurry," the voice said. "Your new life is about to begin."

And no sooner had the voice come than it was taken by the wind and carried away into approaching night. With Carla in his arms Tommy realised, just for one moment, that he sensed everything. He knew the voice had been his voice and it held the vitality of his own creativity. The force of the lines he would write ran through him, through Carla, the mountains and to the vanishing point and beyond. Stories came to him uncluttered with logic. He saw the plots, the characters and some of the dialogue and he knew these would represent the best in his life and the best of his life would remain forever and always with her.

Tommy and Carla moved further down the ridge towards the town. To the right, between gnarled humps, a stream ran. Foam-speckled and tumbling, it cut down beside the path and, at some unseen place, as if playing a game of hide-and-seek, the stream merged into the earth. Tommy took her hand and both disappeared into the gathering darkness and into a wonderland of memories.

*

But the evening of the 3 September 1939 was no respecter of dreams, memories or wonderlands. Silence greeted their arrival in *Giazza*. Even *Perdita di Tempo* was subdued. One of the locals meandered over to tell them what had happened.

"Haven't you heard?"

The man's accusing eyes and his wagging finger told Tommy all he needed to know. The man spoke to Carla and, muttering under his breath, he turned away.

"His says that Britain has declared war on Italy's friend," Carla said. "You cannot be welcome here."

Tommy opened his mouth to say something to the man. But he showed no sign of even wanting to hear Tommy's comment. He was not interested in Tommy. History was not interested in Tommy and history had no time for Carla. All the love in the world was not going to change a thing and he, the spectator of his own unhappiness, was forced to listen to a commentary in his ear and a voice said:

This is the end, Tommy, but in the end, you have your beginning.

10

3 September 1939 - Giazza to Verona

The stone arched through the dusk and landed at his
feet. He watched another flying in the wake of the
first and it crack-landed beside his feet. Both stones had
flown with verbal and non-verbal accompaniment in the
form of jabbing fingers and foul names emanating from
the mouths of schoolboys. They were standing next to
the Alfa and blocking Tommy and Carla's way towards
it. The presence of these boys was a reminder that even
the thugs he had seen in the Communist bar had once
been children. The children in front of him were wearing
black; black shirts, black caps, black shorts and grey
socks and they were chanting in unison. Carla leaned
sideways and whispered in Tommy's ear:

"These boys are following in the footsteps of Luca.
They made inscription with the young Italian Fascists.
They have promised to follow the orders of the *Duce* and
to serve with all their energy the cause of the Fascist
revolution."

Tommy stepped forward to confront these young Fascists, but Carla put a hand on Tommy's shoulder and stopped him in his tracks. The boys were young teenagers and, even in the early evening light, Tommy saw the faces that had mocked them now growing angry. Fortunately, the appearance of the father of one of the boys ended the potential for confrontation.

"The problem is," said Carla, slinging the last of the suitcases onto the back seat, "that they are repeating what they hear from their parents. You English are not wanted here."

It's done, Tommy, it's over.

In a silence of sadness, they drove into the square, past the hotel in which they had danced the tango, past the waving-goodbye-hands of *Perdita di Tempo*, past the church and the hanging flags, out of *Giazza*, down the valley and into the *Val d'Illasi*. And Tommy could only shake his head in disbelief and stifle foul language at his inability to stop the tide, and awareness of his impotence struck him in the stomach and his stomach responded with a sensation of sick dread that soon he and Carla were going to say good bye.

Why us, Tommy? Why does it have to be us?

His shoulders were hunched and his arms were folded. Carla's hands lay tense on the steering wheel. Consumed and separated by a haze of doubts, of love and confusion, they drove down the valley, and Tommy felt out of control and floating from one dark and dumb village to another and nothing could stop this dream-motoring to their end, down the valley and towards the main Verona road and he and Carla were separated by the same nightmare and the same hesitations, doubts and maybes. Maybe he should be staying. Maybe she should be coming to England. Maybe she did not really love him. Maybe he did not love her. Maybe the war would be over by Christmas… Maybe… Maybe… Maybe.

You two have only just started, said the voice in Tommy's ear. It's not fair.

What will happen if I stay?

He was clutching at straws, clutching at a lifebelt, at castles in the air.

You will be arrested as an enemy alien.

What exactly does it mean?

It means you may be suspected of being a spy. It means reporting to the authorities. Perhaps, it means hard labour.

Surely not. I have not committed a crime.

But even as Tommy conversed with himself, he was picturing the black cars appearing outside his hotel in depressing dawn, the men in black shirts emerging and telling him to go with them, telling him it was for his own good.

No, Tommy, the affair is ending. There is nothing you can do.

He looked into the side mirror but saw only darkness behind him and the car droned on towards the darkness of their destiny, and the land flattened out and the silhouettes of castles dominated the skyline until they were back on the plain, in the nightmare, in the agony, the gut-twisting pain.

Will you ever see them again?

Arriving at the hotel, the old man with the whiskers had been replaced by a younger man in a sharp suit but when Tommy told him he would be leaving in the morning, the younger man shook his head.

"We are sorry you are leaving today, but we took the liberty of emptying your room for you. It is for your own safety. We are sure you understand. Your train leaves in 10 minutes."

Now? Now is too soon…it's too soon.

But Tommy left his cases on the back of the car and opened his arms. They held each other, their lips just inches apart and Tommy felt the warm breath of the woman who had changed his life and now he was going to lose her.

*

In later life, Tommy's memory becomes a place in which he often finds shelter, a place he often visits to find peace. He recalls his separation from Carla as a series of well-defined incidents.

She is driving him along *Corso Porta Nuova* towards the train that will take him away. She will park near the station entrance. Tommy feels sick.

Why are you doing this to yourself, Tommy?

I have no choice.

Of course, you have a choice. There is always choice.

But Tommy tells himself that this is the bad dream from which he will never wake, the monster that will never catch him.

And when they arrive at the station, she doesn't switch off the ignition, and the rumble of the Alfa's engine remains in his head. They unpack the car to the sound of it. But she, who has changed him, she, who has set him on a different course, she, who has left the engine running, has one foot in the car and one foot out, caught between coming and going, between wishing and screaming, between wanting him to go and hoping he will stay.

"Well," he says, "see you sometime – when the war is over."

Quick, quick, Tommy, before you have time to weaken - your life is just starting.

But this should not be happening and his brain is telling him that their love is a love lost and a love lost before it is fully formed is a love that never dies and lives on as the haunting grief of what might have been.

"One day, one day I will come back to you. That is a promise… I promise you…Tommy…"

That is the last thing Tommy hears her say but what is her parting shot, the image that torments and obsesses and haunts him? Forever in his thoughts and dreams, she is clutching the edelweiss close to her chest and fingering it while she waves through the smoke. And then the smoke closes around her and she is lost. And he knows that this sense of loss will never leave him.

There are just unwanted voices in his ear:

It is really over.

No, no, I'll be back soon.

No, no, no, it's over.

I'll be back after the war.

No, Tommy, it's over, but seize this moment, this is your beginning.

And somehow, Tommy knows it is meant to be. He will never see her again.

PART 2

June - July 1990. Hampton Court,
England and Verona, Italy

11

27 June 1990 - Hampton Court, England

Tommy turned his face from breeze to sun and from sun to breeze. The breeze stroked his cheeks, curled around his ear and nose and flirted with his hair. But the sun gave him warmth, filled every line, wrinkle and crease on his face and energised him.

It was a BBC Radio news announcement that stopped him mid-turn. Until the announcement, the radio had emitted soft rock and melodies that sounded from the kitchen to reach him on the balcony. It seemed that the British author Salman Rushdie, condemned to death by Iran, had donated $8.600 to its earthquake victims. Tommy allowed the news to sink into his head, his head to sink into the cushion and reflected on Rushdie's death sentence in particular and death sentences in general and concluded that everybody lived with a death sentence hanging over them and that such a terminal condition should deter everybody from shilly-shallying and dithering.

Di-the-ring. What a wonderful word.

He loved its suggestions of old England and regional dialects. He wondered if it were related to the word "dodder" or "dodderer." Unfortunately, both words applied to him.

Tommy, my boy, you are the archetypal dithering old dodderer.

It had to be age that was the source of his indecision, he thought. Age forced those afflicted by it to act on whims. Nobody made long-term plans at the age of seventy. You could be late and lamented well before the start date.

Tommy closed his eyes and turned his face to the sunlight. The wail of a lovelorn singer emerged from the kitchen to compete with the sound of a passenger jet roaring to its cruising altitude from Heathrow. Its engine note was the giveaway. Landing jets were quieter unless you were living underneath them. The heat of the sun encouraged his mind to fly up with the silver bird and away with it to Verona, perhaps, where she would be waiting for him. Tommy shook his head again and, pushing himself to a sitting position, he sucked air through his back teeth.

"For God's sake."

He straddled the sunbed and rested his feet on the balcony floor.

"You really are a bloody idiot, man."

It was indeed idiotic to think that, even if he went back, he would find her there. True, Tommy knew that the world was in constant motion and it was feasible that if he sat on the same spot long enough, and with a patience he did not possess, he might meet Carla again. After all, she might be looking for him.

"Pah… That won't be happening."

The notion was preposterous. He was not the person to sit in one place for long and nor had Carla been. Tommy let his head drop into his hands.

Nor had Carla been. You used the past perfect tense, Tommy.

Tommy turned his head into the breeze.

And why shouldn't I? She would have been killed in the war.

Carla had been Jewish. It was not unreasonable to assume that she had been murdered 50 years earlier in the camps.

Tommy turned his face to the sunlight.

That is no reason not to revisit the place, and see it again for one last time.

"One last time? God's teeth."

You may not be writing novels these days, old chap, but you haven't lost your tendency for the melodramatic, have you?

The words did sound exaggerated. Once upon a time, he had spent one week in Verona and its surroundings. So, at that time and in that week his life had changed. But he had now reached a point in his life in which he would change no more. Revisiting the past could not alter a thing. But looking up to watch the net curtains brushing against the window frames, he knew he was going to go. His vacillations and doubts and misgivings were a sham. The decision was made. A slow process, that had started on a whim several days earlier, had ended in firmness of purpose.

Come on, Tommy, what have you got to lose? Only your life perhaps, and that has already been lived. Go and get it out of your system.

Thomas Mostyn, known as "Tommy" to his few friends, knew and accepted that he was at the end of the road. These days, nobody telephoned to ask after Tommy or to ask what Tommy was up to. Nobody, apart from the postman, rang his doorbell, and his letters were not of the social kind. They were mostly bills or demands for money he did not have. If he passed away today, nobody except debt collectors would ask where Tommy had gone and they would find that he had left precious little money behind him.

He had even noticed that other regulars at the Kings Arms no longer appeared for a pint and a chin-wag. It never occurred to Tommy that they might be dead. Nor did it ever cross his mind that they were put off by the increasing number of tourists. Privatisation of the palace had resulted in a marketing plan, entrance prices and hordes of tourists exiting the palace grounds by the Lion Gate where the Kings Arms stood waiting to fulfil their bodily needs.

Nonetheless, the huge number of tourists at Hampton Court Palace did not explain why his publisher was ignoring him. Tommy had to face the truth. His glory days were long gone, his books were out of vogue and nobody read them.

There was a knock on the door.

"Mr Mostyn, sir. Mr Mostyn."

It was the caretaker.

"You at home, sir?"

Damn the man's eyes. Not now. Why couldn't he leave an old man alone to enjoy the sunshine in peace?

"A letter for you, sir, and it looks important."

"Be so good as to slip it under the door, would you?" Tommy said.

There was a pause and a rustle. The rustle was long enough for Tommy to reflect that he was being unfair. The caretaker was a kind man and he seemed to care for the cantankerous old gaffer living on the second floor.

Well, maybe it is time the young man learned that being caring and kind does not make you many friends.

There was a sound of paper rubbing between door and carpet.

"Could be an old flame, sir."

The young caretaker was attempting a joke, a flame to brighten Tommy's day.

"An old flame?" Tommy said, more to himself than to the caretaker. "Not much chance of that, son."

His wife had been the last woman in his life and she had left years ago. And before that? He had known many women but none of them had stayed the course. He did not blame them. Writing novels had been an all-consuming passion and his existence had been self-centred – but not always. Once upon a time, and it was a long time ago, he had been open enough to experience real love. In the summer of 1939, there had been an earnest youth. On a mountain top, this youth and a young Italian woman had danced the tango and made love - once upon a time. But where now was the burning Italian sun? Where was that Tango? Where now was the intimacy they had shared?

"Fifty years have passed by," Tommy whispered. "That's where it's gone."

Much to Tommy's disgust, the porter had not gone with it.

"Sir, sir? Doesn't seem to fit, sir. You'll need to open the door, sir."

Tommy leaned forward and, with a push of his thighs, he rose to his feet and steadied himself.

"Tottering old dodderer," he muttered while turning to face the sitting-room.

He put one hand on the sliding glass door and the other hand on the balcony wall. Well-balanced, and with his arms spread out in crucifixion, he poked his head into the sitting-room.

"Leave it on the doormat, then," he said.

"No can do, sir," the porter said. "Special delivery, sir. Must ensure the letter crosses the threshold. It's the rules, sir."

Tommy blew with impatience, shuffled across the room to the front door and pulled at the bolts and levers that might stop burglars from getting in but also stopped him from getting out.

"Surprised to find you at home, sir. Thought you'd gone to Italy, sir."

"Italy?"

"Italy, sir. Told me last week, sir."

Tommy shook his head. His brain must resemble a slice of *Emmental* cheese with ever increasing numbers of holes down which his memory was sinking.

"Yes, sir. Told me all about her, sir. Said love had never died, sir. Said that you went back after the war to find her. Lovely story, if you don't mind me saying so, sir."

Tommy raised his eyebrows. It was true that he had never accepted that the love he had once felt had faded to nothing more than a pleasant memory. He had accepted that his world and Carla's had become separated by more than time. They had walked the same road for a short while and then, when war broke out, the road had forked and they had gone separate ways – he to a life as a warrior and writer and she almost certainly to a concentration camp and death.

"I don't mind you saying so," Tommy said while throwing back the last bolt.

He had, indeed, returned after the war to look for her but how could the young porter understand the extent of the war damage and connected difficulties he faced in 1945? No amount of love could repair the bridges and buildings of his memory. No amount of dedication could remove the tens of thousands of displaced persons who, like Tommy, were looking for loved ones. The Red Cross and other relief organisations did all they could to help him but the situation for Jews was complicated. Many of them did not have homes, families or communities to go back to. On top of that, there were so many "maybes." Maybe she had changed her name. Maybe she had gone to Israel or South America. And what about the "mights?" She might have joined a partisan group during the hostilities. She might have died during a firefight. She might have died in a hospital, a displacement camp, a cave in a forest or a mountainside. She might, in fact, be almost anywhere or nowhere on the planet.

Tommy's front door eventually swung open to reveal a small and squarely-built young man with a chained pocket-watch buried in a waistcoat pocket and a large brown envelope cradled in his arms. When the young man leaned forward with the envelope between his hands, Tommy was almost expecting to hear the words: "Sir, is your majesty willing to take this letter?"

Tommy took the envelope from the caretaker's outstretched hands and the man said:

"Must have loved her, sir, if you don't mind me suggesting it, sir. Know what they say, sir? Time mends a broken heart. Did you go back and look for her again?"

Tommy remained silent for a short while. It was a silence that was intended to communicate that it was nobody's business whether or not he had ever set foot in Italy again. Nonetheless, he shook his head.

"No, I didn't go back," Tommy said. "But, you know, memory endures for a while."

For many years after the war, Tommy had turned, expecting to see Carla behind him and hoping to gaze into those big brown eyes. Time passed, the swinging sixties arrived, and other women took Carla's place. But Tommy was delighted to find that Carla's memory was already a habit to him, and when he gazed into the distance, he caught sight of her, the dark wavy hair, the alabaster skin and those big eyes. Yes, memory endured but eventually memory faded and bits of Carla dropped away – at first the exact shape of the nose, and then the ears and the pouting lips and finally the smell of her until, by the middle of the eighties when his writing lost its public appeal, the fading reached a tipping point. The name "Carla" became a word without a clear thought and words without clear thoughts were dead things and this dead thing was attached to a blurred image of a girl, a mist of indeterminate shape and colour.

"And I was very busy writing books."

And he could have added that his books could never have been written without the memory of Carla. Her soul haunted everything he had ever written and, in a very real sense, everything he had written was a love letter to her, and while his books were being read, she was immortal. All this offered real consolation until the day, horror of horrors, that book sales began to drop off and memories of her wore thin. But then what could one expect?

"Well, 50 years have passed since my Verona days," Tommy said.

"Long time, sir."

"Indeed, it is."

Or were those years just a dream?

Tommy sighed. What was the point in regrets and dreaming? Reality was the damned letter in his hand, books that no longer made any sales, money he no longer had and bills that had to be paid. Looking down at the envelope, Tommy was appalled at its bigness, its ugliness. It would contain a big demand for big money or yet another big and ugly bill he was unable to pay. It lay in the palm of his hand like the day of judgement. Its colour – official government brown – was threatening, filled him with dread and reinforced an idea that he had been flirting with since seeing a performance of *Hamlet* at the palace earlier in the year. The young prince's problem had become his. "To be or not to be? That is the question."

To put it another way, do you really need this crap at this time of your life or should you have one last Italian holiday, come home and put an end to it all? That is now the question you have to answer, old chap.

12

27 June 1990 - Hampton Court, England

Tommy glared at the envelope in his hand. A variety of feelings and thoughts-in-progress rippled from his forehead, down through his cheeks and into his mouth. The thoughts emerged as two plosives, one voiceless sibilant and a simple comment.

"Pah. Bull. Shit. I don't need these people."

"Sorry, sir?"

"Oh, my apologies," Tommy said, indicating the name and logo of the law firm stamped above the envelope window. "I was simply referring to the senders of the letter."

No, he didn't need brown envelopes from solicitors politely making demands for money and he would not allow them to shame him.

"I see, sir."

"Always demanding money."

"Yes, sir."

The caretaker's round face was shining along with the glass in his spectacles.

If you have to go, Tommy, go with dignity and not as a man reduced to shadows, a down-and-out relic, thrown out of his lodgings, roaming the streets and looking for somewhere to sleep while being chased by creditors like these legal people.

"Excuse me, sir, but you have got my imagination working overtime. Can I ask another question, sir?"

Tommy glanced towards the bottle of barbiturates. The pills were fast and painless and they stood in waiting, the final solution beside the whisky bottle.

"Ask away," he said.

"It possible that she is still alive, sir?"

"Is it possible? Yes," he said. "Is it probable? No."

Tommy muttered a string of obscenities at the law firm and held the envelope away from his body as if it were contaminated. He carried the envelope to the sideboard and dropped it next to the whisky bottle. Then, imitating a chess-game castling move he snapped up both the barbiturate bottle and the whisky bottle in one hand and brought them down hard on the envelope. Priorities had to be maintained.

"You going back to look for her, sir?"

"Good lord, no."

"Well, I was just thinking sir."

"Yes?"

"Well, sir, you said you were going back to Italy, sir? Why not Spain or France, sir?"

Because it's a sort of summing up.

It was also a reassessment of a time and a place in which he felt he had experienced true happiness through love. And Tommy already pictured himself shadowing the footsteps of his younger self and looking for a pinch of understanding concerning this most elusive of emotional states. He had often theorised that happiness was a retrospective phenomenon.

Did you really experience the delights that memory suggests or is the past like the photographs in glossy magazines?

Tommy knew that these photos were often edited and the final product was like his books - a fiction. In comparison with these edited pictures, the present would always look shabby and the future would always look bleak. Essentially, his question was simple.

Was that time in Verona a sham, a touched-up memory and a myth that never quite happened?

He was aware of the dangers of going to Verona. To discover that he had been living on myths would not be easy to take. His memories of Carla, his love for her and pre-war Verona were the most sacred he possessed and they were a part of his identity. He had experienced first love but he had also witnessed violence and there had been fear and uncertainty and decisions to make. In the end, he had walked away of his own free will.

But at least we were spared those crushing experiences, those moments of absence and guilt – absence of desire, and guilt because the flame was out.

"Why Italy? I know my way around in Italy," Tommy said. "And I don't speak Spanish or French."

"But she might be still alive, sir. If I may be so bold, sir, why did you not go back again before, I mean, when things had settled down after the war?"

Because you could never face the strong possibility that she was dead, could you, Tommy old boy? For the sake of your books and the sake of your sanity, you needed to know that she could be somewhere on this planet, reading your books and yearning for you.

"Because," Tommy said, "by 1945 between 62 and 78 million people lost their lives as a result of the Second World War. They died on the battlefield. They were killed by aerial bombs. They were murdered in death camps. About half of those who died were civilians. Carla was a civilian and Carla was a Jew. Now, if you don't mind…"

"Certainly, sir. Please don't hesitate to ask me if you need anything, sir."

The caretaker did a sort of bow and stepped backwards away from the door, turned smartly and clattered down the stairs. Tommy heard his footsteps fade away until the front door of the man's basement flat closed with a crash.

Yes, Tommy, old chap, you needed the possibility that at some point and at some place you would meet again, didn't you?

In fact, Tommy had spent many happy hours lost in daydreams and imagining the possible scenarios: an accidental meeting with Carla in the palace grounds, the sight of her across the breakfast room in some hotel in Spain and these scenarios inspired him. One day, in late September the previous year, he believed he had actually seen her for the first and last time. It was a Sunday morning and he was strolling over Hampton Court Bridge when he thought he saw her walking along the towpath and he set off in pursuit. The palace itself was materialising through a thin fog which had been hanging over the river as a harbinger of autumn since the early morning. Down by the waterside, the fog was thick enough to obscure the opposite bank of the river.

There was a dredger, a shifting shadow, under Hampton Court Bridge and its full mechanical booms and rattlings were dampened by the mist and drifting over the river towards him. He watched her walking through the wispy arms of white that reached out to grip those, like her, who might be walking on the river's edge.

Further along the path, he was distracted by the arrival of the first passenger boat from Kingston. With a shudder of reversing propellers, the boat thumped against the wooden jetty. The ropes were then thrown and tied, and the deck hands stood to one side to allow the passengers to spill down the gangplank and gather in groups on the towpath. Tommy joined the groups as they funnelled through a heavy, wrought-iron gate that led into the palace grounds.

Suddenly, shockingly, she was gone.

In desperation, he took a left-hand path and approached the rose garden. From nearby tennis courts came the pock, pock, of racket against ball. The sound echoed in the stillness of the garden. Disembodied shouts encouraged and congratulated, and from a not-too-distant radio, the sound of music drifted across the lawns. But Carla – or she, who looked like Carla - had disappeared. Again. Forever.

Tommy stepped onto his balcony, sat on his sunbed, lay back, and settled his head on the cushion and closed his eyes. This time, his head remained still.

You are, or you were, a writer, Tommy. And writers don't live in a world of truth or lies. You needed the fantasy that Carla was alive. Better a happy fantasy than an unhappy truth, Tommy. That just about explains it all, doesn't it? Your writer's soul needed the idea of Carla rather than Carla herself.

The advantages of being old brought an outline of a smile to Tommy's face. Old age was not just about physical decline. The imminent arrival of the "grim reaper" severely restricted not only his future prospects but also future penalties.

Why give your last pennies to your creditors, Tommy? You can spend them on something more pleasurable – a trip back in time – a last goodbye, for example. And when you return? The barbiturates will be waiting.

What he needed to do in Italy was to review and evaluate, to put to rest, to say goodbye. Then he could

come back to England and die in peace and by own
hand.

13

24 July1990 – on the train to Verona

He blinked at his watch. A glance through the window confirmed his suspicion that he had daydreamed away the Brenner. Not only was the train swishing downwards to *Vipiteno*, something different, something Italian, was in the air. He sniffed at it and sensed this shift from an indoor world of musty air, tea and ticking clocks to an outdoor world of sunlight, shadow and openness. The sun's warmth pricked at Tommy's face and he saw lightness of being on the bodies of his fellow travellers, their inclusive and expansive arm movements expressing the inexpressible and he heard it in the tumbling of their talk, rapid and excited speech accompanied by the wagging of chins, the raising of fingers, the hunching of shoulders and arms open to welcome the light and to feel the day.

Tommy leaned forward. Looking through the window, he noted how, despite their rapid descent, everything seemed to pass by in slow motion. Then, they plunged into a tunnel, the lights flickered on, the door slid open at the far end of his carriage and two uniformed men came through. Their arm movements suggested they were demanding travel tickets; their leg movements suggested restless urgency, but they dragged their heels, looking into each bay of seats and glancing into the faces of each passenger while light bounced off their bald heads when they passed under the ceiling lamps, and the swish of the train became muted as if everything was covered in snow.

Tommy shivered. Big men in uniforms, speaking Italian and making demands brought back nightmarish memories of Fascist Verona, 1939: the point of the blade sliding into the skin under the chin, reappearing in the mouth and striking the palate. The events of that time were so extreme, so dark, that without his memory to tell him it was true, it would be unimaginable. Tommy had little doubt that the perpetrators had never been identified and tried in Italy whereas most of the witnesses would have worked hard at forgetting what they had seen and they would never have shared it with anyone. But then, neither had he.

Then, the train was racing out of the darkness and back into the light, the vine terraces and the trees dripping with ripening apples, and whooshing through villages with bars and men playing cards, women dressed in black selling vegetables dressed in light, and between mountain and villages were the hills, a van glinting in the silver of olive groves, cypress trees lending their shadows to patterns on the hilltops. Everything was awash with sunlight.

Inside the carriage, in the wake of the ticket inspectors, came the trolley of snacks and Tommy bought a cheese roll and a bottle of white wine and the compartment filled at every stop with gesturing, chattering excitement and by the time the train screeched to a halt at Trento, Tommy was exchanging questions and answers with complete strangers.

"Why are you here?"

"What do you do?"

"Come and visit us."

"We can show you around."

"I am Tommy Mostyn and I am a novelist," he said.

"What are you writing?"

"What have you written?"

"Are you married?"

"Do you have children?"

Are you still a famous novelist, Tommy?

Only those who were old enough and lonely enough to scour the quality newspaper obituaries for comfort might pause at the insertion: *Suddenly on 10 August 1990, Thomas Mostyn, novelist, aged 70 – at home, Hampton Court.*

It tickled him to think that these words would be relevant only to those people in search of reassurance at some familiar name they had outlived. And who could say what they would associate with his name. Early promise fallen victim to mediocrity? In their eyes, his life had, perhaps, been reduced to that of a faded writer, a "has-been" who had appeared for an instant, joined a community of other scribblers and, without a whimper, had passed on.

He didn't tell these adoring fellow travellers that his work was out of time. His publisher had been left with the task of telling him, and the telling of it had felt like betrayal. Tommy had tried in vain to explain that updating the true love story was his attempt at something original, something that would appeal to people for whom cheap flights and a greater variety of holiday destinations were the new norm. His publisher's position was that the modern age had the opposite effect. Who needed to read about true love in exotic and faraway places when you could experience them yourself?

But one lie led to another.

"Are you working on a novel now?"

"Of course," Tommy said. "Actually, I am on my way to Verona to feel its history."

"Oh," they said. "And what is the book about?"

"It's a love story."

There was a collective "coo" of pleasure and a multitude of fingertips tugging at lower eyelids and a chorus of comments and questions.

"In Verona?"

"Is the city of love…"

"When we can buy the book?"

Tommy was disturbed by the fact that to every question, there was an answer and the answers came out so naturally that they sounded true – even to him. The reality was that after the rift with his publisher, he had gone into a permanent depressive state. Gone was the belief in himself. Dead was the desire to write that definitive work for which he would be forever revered. Doubt replaced his trust in the future to bring about change. The future had arrived and he was staring at it from the shadows, hopelessly staring and thinking in the darkness. He was written out. That definitive work would never be written and further thoughts would remain forever wordless.

"I had a girlfriend in Verona," he said to one old lady. "A long time ago. In fact, it was before the war."

The old lady was tall and gaunt and with rouge on her lips and cheeks and blue streaks in her hair. Despite the warmth, she was wearing a light black coat and she constantly touched and shifted the position of her glasses as if she were changing their focus.

"Ah… A long time ago. What was her name?"

"Her name was Carla."

The old lady nodded wisely and pulled at her glasses.

"And when did you last see Carla?"

"It was the day war was declared in September 1939."

The old lady nodded again and studied him over the rim of her spectacles.

"Would you recognise Carla if you saw her again?"

Tommy had often asked himself this very question. In many ways she had been reduced to a slender and narrow shape waving to him as his train left Verona in 1939. He had leaned far out of the window until she was a speck amongst other specks in the distance. The world around him was falling apart and not because of the war but because he had wanted to reach out and touch the alabaster of her skin for once last time.

"Yes," he said. "I would recognise her immediately."

The old lady got up to leave and touched his hand with hers. It lingered there for a long time.

"Do you know what we say about first love?"

Tommy looked up and into her eyes and, at that moment, he had a vision of Carla, almost saw her as if she were beside him in a dream. And with the dream-image came the light sparkling on the river *Adige* and dancing on the pink Verona marble, and he heard the breathing of the city as a distant and indistinct murmur between the church towers, the Roman remains and the hills and the shadows. He had, in fact, been expecting to see shadows of Carla since they crossed the Brenner.

There had been suggestions of her alabaster skin and her brown eyes in the skin and eyes of others. But the real vision came to him in the manner of a conjuring trick with the old lady's question about first love. Along with the light, the people and the smells of Italy, he received a strong sense of himself as he had been back then - a young man, fresh from school and on a mini grand tour organised and paid for by his father. Tommy had been 19, absorbed in a book, and on his way to

Verona. But so distant was that place where memory beckoned that he could never be sure. Who was that person he saw in his mind's eye? Who was the young man, snug by the window and isolated from the world?

Is that me as I was in 1939 that I see now in my mind's eye. Or is that me, the aged man, the 70-year-old I see in the mirror on those days I decide to shave?

He recalled the train, or perhaps the idea of a train, rushing all the way from 1939 like a smell-induced memory. The *Padana* plain had been wreathed in mist and although the compartment was warm, it seemed dingy and damp and the light was yellow and sombre. The confrontation with Luca had been reduced to the idea of pain in his jaw but he would never forget her skin and those big brown eyes.

The old lady's voice was in his ear and her hand pressuring his.

"Well? Do you know what they say about first love?"

Tommy shook his head.

"Sorry," he said. "I was far away."

"First love does not forget," she said.

She made a movement that suggested she would turn away and then changed her mind. She removed her glasses and said rather dramatically:

"No, never."

She looked into his eyes and then she was gone, floating down the gangway while the seated passengers leaned sideways so as not to touch when she passed. Tommy lost sight of her amongst the passengers mingling by the exit doors and he stared through the train window at the vineyards and the unfolding *Padana* plain and asked himself how accurate his memory of Carla was. Had their affair really been the way he remembered or was he replaying selected parts in his memory and adding bits that never happened? And what of those parts that had been forgotten? It had taken him 3 days to find the guts to phone her.

The passengers were rising from their seats, fumbling for their luggage and staggering down the corridor. Brakes were squealing, balance was lost, bodies were bumped, apologies were uttered and crowds were forming by the exit doors. Tommy remained seated. He recognised the hills that rose behind the city. They were the same green hills he had seen 50 years before and they were still crowned with the darker green of cypress trees and rose over the city, its porticos, its crenellations, its gardens and statues coming and going with the speed of the train and the whish and the whoosh, the clatter and the squeal and the cries of the vendors, the whispers of love and the wails of despair at Juliet's balcony.

Tommy sidled down the train corridor to join the people at the door. He closed his eyes for a moment and drifted back to September 1939 when he had witnessed violence and murder, when he had fallen into love, and a lifetime of doubts and what-ifs had followed. He was still dreaming when he stepped down from the carriage. He was fantasising when his foot fell incorrectly on the folding steps. He was putting out his arms to steady himself when he realised, he had been half-expecting to see her rooted to the spot on which he had last seen her 50 years before. But it was already too late. He was lurching sideways, falling through the air and past images of he and Carla on their terrace in the sun, the faces of the people around him, the faces of Fascist black-shirts chasing him through the streets of the city, the arms stretched out towards him and he sailed further towards the station platform and landed on his back like an upturned beetle.

14

24 – 27 July 1990 – Verona

Tommy had not expected his return to Verona to draw a crowd, but an elderly man lurching to one side and falling heavily on his back was enough to raise concern amongst fellow travellers. Within seconds, and amidst a chaos of body language, garlic breath and Italian chatter, a variety of people were worrying and fretting and lifting him to his feet. Someone brushed his jacket, a woman tutted and others stood sentinel beside his luggage.

"*Sto bene,*" Tommy said.

Using two Italian words he had learned from Carla some 50 years before pleased Tommy so much that he decided to add a third.

"*Sto bene, veramente…*"

Tommy took several steps forward to show the crowd that he really was OK and used gestures to demonstrate that he could walk unaided.

Expect a bruise though, Tommy, my boy.

By the time the chattering had ceased and the crowd melted away, Tommy had taken the first hit of confusion - the contradiction between what had been preserved in his memory since September 1939 and the current station, a modernist construction of white marble. Gone was the central dome, the two smaller buildings on either side, the waiting-room and the buffet. Even the mosaics had been plundered.

Get a grip, Tommy, and do not allow this to ruin your holiday.

After all, 50 years had gone by since he last set foot on Verona *Porta Nuova* station and in those 50 years, the city had been transformed by World War 2 in general, by several allied bombing raids and by strategic destruction by German defenders in particular.

He got into a taxi, left his initial disappointments at the station, and while the Fiat sped through the streets, he reflected that his happiest memories lived in this town and these gave him both a right of ownership and a right to comment on change. His memories were connected to an era of promise, to the dreams of 1930s youth, to alternative political orders and to change. He and his generation had sung the songs of hope, but he and his friends had also fought a war, had died, had aged and vanished.

But Carla hasn't vanished, Tommy, and don't you forget it. She has remained in the thirties.

She was beautiful to him, and her beauty had not worn as he had worn. For a moment, he believed he could see himself as he had been in 1939. Unmolested by fifty years, he was nineteen, absorbed in himself, and at the centre of the universe. But so distant was that place where memory called that he could never be sure.

Tommy muttered a string of curses and looked up. In 1939, he had come here as a young man and fallen in love. And yet, as the taxi rumbled over the cobbled streets in 1990, Tommy found himself just a couple of strides ahead of an uncomfortable thought. It followed him past the church of *San Fermo* and caught up with him soon after crossing the *Adige* river.

Time has moved on, Tommy. Your memories may live here, but you are now a stranger in your own dreams. Do not forget this.

Nonetheless, he did not even try to stifle a smile when he saw that the Hotel Arena was still being squeezed between the Roman gateway on one side and the building that had once housed the offices of regional administration on the other. That construction was now a library and the hotel itself seemed distorted as if collapsing under its own weight, but even more bizarre was the manager, Signor Caruso. His twisted body suggested he had adapted to his environment in sympathy.

"I stayed here for a few days before the war," Tommy said.

Caruso exaggerated a shrug and said:

"A long time ago."

"Indeed, it was," said Tommy. "Do you happen to have the register from that time, August 1939? I would like to see…"

The manager smiled faintly.

"Destroyed," he said.

"After the war?" Tommy suggested.

"Exactly, signor Mostyn, a long time ago."

"Indeed, it is a long time ago."

"Our hotel is as respectable now as it was then," Caruso said with a movement of the cheeks that suggested a smile. "*Fascisti* were not welcome in the past years and they are not welcome today. I am sure you understand."

He handed Tommy his key.

"Customers are our number 1 priority. Please enjoy the opera," he said.

"I am not here to go to the opera," Tommy said with an imitation smile of his own. "I am here to write."

Tommy stared at Caruso open-mouthed. He had not intended to use these words but there they were, spoken entirely on impulse and hanging in the air between them.

When was the last time you said you had to write, Tommy? Was it so long ago that you no longer remember?

"Enjoy," Caruso said.

After unpacking, Tommy took the stairs down to the breakfast balcony and into a place where other memories had been entombed and worshipped.

And probably embellished – a sprinkling of rose petals here, a frame of Bougainvillea there and perfumed with flowers and enjoyed to the backdrop of the Adige river.

His terrace in the sun was alive and dancing with sunlight and it could so easily have been the same sunlight that had bathed him and Carla that morning in the late summer of 1939. Umbrellas were still domed and protective, Bougainvillea was still cascading down the side of the building and the terrace walls were blushing in response. And at his feet, and still tumbling and running through the bridges, was the *Adige* river.

He ordered coffee from an inattentive man in a white jacket and sat staring at the foam-specked waters of the *Adige* remembering the day he had met Carla on the train. Something had passed between them - a look, or was it the note or her body language and a challenge to use her invitation and ring her. And why them? Because they happened to be on the same train at the same time and because she was daring enough to write him that note and because it was him and because it was her and the thought made Tommy reach for a pencil and he noted it down on the back of his bill before the thought disappeared into a big, black hole.

He walked out of the hotel, along *Via Cappello* and towards *Piazza delle Erbe*. Skirting the crowds outside Juliet's balcony, he strolled into the square, which was as busy now as it had been 50 years previously when he had used the place as a stage to test his "look" but the reality now was that nobody was looking in his direction and this was no surprise to him given that he was now a non-being, a one-size-fits-all stereotype, an alien with physical and mental disablements. In other words, he was old and even though, occasionally, the real person inside came flashing out, only he was there to listen to his voice and this voice was urging him to feel the city and its history developing in front of his eyes.

But he felt this determination weaken when he strode into *Piazza Bra*. He could not shake off Carla's ghost. The flowers there could so easily have been the same flowers they had seen in late summer 1939. Tommy even crossed into the sunlight as Carla would have done and felt the warmth on his shoulders as she would have felt it, for the day was as long then as now and the shadows were as short.

Wandering into a garden in the middle of the square, Tommy stopped to listen. Carla had loved birds and birdsong and their song was now deafening. It was almost as if they knew autumn was coming and found the strength to celebrate its advent with one last hurrah. It might even have been the same birds, Tommy thought, and he glimpsed that timeless world in which past and present were one while digging into his pocket for the bill.

That's good, Tommy, yes, I like that.

He borrowed a pencil from a crossword-puzzler sitting on a nearby bench and added to the notes he had already made. He fingered the pencil while gazing at the knots of elderly men who had gathered in the garden. He started scribbling notes while reflecting that these old men could have been the sons and grandsons of the men that he had seen in 1939. They were merrily chatting and they orchestrated their conversation with expansive gestures while children jumped and scurried around them. Mothers were still crying out: "*Antonio, Antonio, vieni Antonio,*" and as Tommy walked out of the garden and back into the square, the cries followed him, long drawn out and despairing like a faraway train whistling in the night. And all the time, Tommy wanted to say:

"Come out, Carla, come out wherever you are. I don't want to play this game of hide-and-seek anymore. Please, come out."

But there was nobody there to answer him. He sat down on a nearby bench and tried to find some acceptance. He became aware that his eyelids were drooping and revealing a face, a familiar face which touched some memory to which he could put neither place nor time. Sensing a presence behind him, Tommy turned and saw a figure approaching from the *Liston*. The figure came relentlessly on until, just short of him, it stopped. It was the old, tall and gaunt woman with whom he had conversed on the train and she was staring at Tommy as if she were annoyed at finding him there.

"You again. Why are you sitting there like this?" she said. "You have so little time."

Tommy sat stock still as a gentle breeze picked up and blew between them. There was something about her that matched neither his expectation nor his experience and she was still wearing the light black coat but she appeared to look through him as if he was not really there.

"You need to get started right now," she said. "Get started now before it's too late."

Tommy remained silent. This stranger from the train had no past, no future and was unrelated to everything he knew and yet as he sat there, he felt, just for one moment, that he understood everything. He had been ignoring it, refusing to believe he could do it, had lost direction and faith in it, when, all the time, it had been there patiently waiting for him to pick it up again.

Shuffling from side to side, Tommy fingered at his jacket for a pen and paper, and the woman continued to stare through him. She took a step sideways and walking past she brushed his shoulder. On impulse, Tommy put out his hand and gently touched her arm but she brushed him off and disappeared. Tommy woke with a start, slapped his thigh and shook his head.

"Get a grip, man," he said to himself, and he jumped up and went in search of a stationers.

Tommy found one not far from *Piazza delle Erbe* and he bought a blue leather-bound book of fine quality paper and a propelling pencil with HB leads. He had always loved this combination. It was ideal for writing, smooth and with a low smudging level. Above all, it gripped the paper and he loved the gentle sound of scratching out the words from his memory.

Clutching the writing book and the pencil, he made his way out of the shop and into *Corso Borsari*. Tommy had expected Verona to be waiting for him and in a sense, it was. Walking into *Corso Cavour* he realised that fragments of Carla were scattered over the city like graffiti. He repeatedly saw her in the crowds that snaked through the streets, past *Castelvecchio* and into *Via Roma* and no matter that it was just Carla's resemblance passing across anonymous faces like a cloud and no matter that he felt untouchable because his feelings were unique and special, he felt that overpowering need to write to her again and he felt extraordinarily happy and light of foot and, more than this, life was resuming its normality and carrying on as usual and the price of coffee or a hotel room did not change because a man had found he was still a little bit in love with a ghost from his past and he dreamed about her while napping on benches and saw her face in the faces of others.

He made towards an empty chair on the pavement outside *Bar Castello*, ordered coffee and sat down to write. He was still there, several glasses of wine and plates of sandwiches later. He was still there and scribbling in his notebook when the bar closed and the lights went out.

15

On the second day, he lingered on the hotel terrace to read through his notes and story outline from the previous day. Occasionally, he felt inspiration and allowed himself to get carried away both with its demands and the feel of the propelling pencil with its HP leads carving out the rhythm of his story. Around midday, his writing stalled when he needed details that only a visit would satisfy. He snapped the notebook shut, tucked the pencil into its spine, and trotted down the stairs and into the street.

He sensed rather than remembered that he was following his own ghost along *Stradone San Fermo* and into *Piazza Bra*. He floated over his 1939 footsteps and he still had a memory of himself as he had been at that time. Muscular and taut, he had been carried forward by his youth.

Running blindly, he had felt his way to a meeting with destiny.

Tommy paused, stood in the shadow of a bar and scribbled down these thoughts in his leather-bound note book, reread them and shook his head and erased them while recalling the evening they had met, her eyes, the clutch bag – flared and white – and the way she occasionally pulled it towards her stomach and fingered it with the other hand.

Was she really wearing those boyish clothes which exaggerated her shoulders and made her legs look so long?

He shook his head.

Probably not, Tommy. It is highly likely that you dressed her in those clothes at some later point – Tommy the costume designer dressing his leading lady.

And when they had introduced themselves, Tommy had always told himself that there had been a warmth in her hand, a surge of electricity. Now he was having doubts. Perhaps, he was creating myths that would convince him that, once upon a time, he had been happy. Perhaps, there had been no electricity and no warmth. Perhaps he had been totally wrapped up in himself and they had been just another couple in a crowded bar.

The thought made him shake his head.

No, Tommy. It was not like that.

Short and special was how it was, with the future some faraway place, and the present all such newness that there was no time for the experiences to settle, no time to reflect and feel, and nor had there been time to project their lives and feel desire and yearning.

In fact, even at the time, both he and Carla had known that their story would be short and the thought of the end underpinned their time even though they ignored it or put the idea out of reach but even in the mountains, they had been followed by these bad dreams and Tommy knew that all dreams were made of things from the waking world and in the waking world their dreams would come to rest. After all, where now was that electric charge, that pain of fleeting joy?

He searched for the Communist Bar in the area beside the *Liston* but there was no sign of any bar. Most of the old had gone and had been replaced by the new - a supermarket, an office block and a bank. What he did recall was the face looking back at him from across the table and the skin like alabaster. He recalled the hush after the gun went off and the blade entering the throat and two men who died. It all seemed so pointless now.

Fishing in his pocket for some change, Tommy bought a paper from a kiosk and took it to the piazza. There were encouraging open-for-business sounds and the odour of fresh coffee and pastry drifted towards him. He tossed the paper and his notebook on a table top and sat down. A breeze was blowing from the mountains and brushed against his cheek. Turning, he saw, away in the distance, on the brow of a hill, a building with yellow-ochre walls and a red roof. The building was so old it appeared to grow naturally out of the ground like the cypress trees that surrounded it. Beyond these trees he saw the circle of the Dolomite Alps set against the skyline. Then, when he was least expecting it, he was 19 again and out came her face, the pleasure and the pain.

"Here we are," the memories said, "you thought we had disappeared, didn't you? But you? You can never forget."

Somewhere a radio was playing a song he had heard from years gone by. The song had been updated but it was still being sung to a tango rhythm.

"Forget me," sang the singer, "forget me as a sad memory that each holds in the heart with the secret ache... Forget me…"

Tommy shook his head.

No chance, mate. Forgetting is not the answer.

He opened his notebook and, placing it on his knees he began to write. No sooner had be started than a waiter appeared to ask for his order. Left alone, Tommy looked at what he had written, "…because it was you…" He heard the rattling of cup against saucer from some place over his shoulder. When the waiter arrived, he was an outline seen from the corner of Tommy's eye. He glimpsed the whiteness of an apron and he noticed the tray swinging down by the man's side when he placed the rattling cup on the table. Tommy hardly noticed the waiter turning away but he was aware of his own hand poised in the air as if he were stalking a fly. Then, he sprung. He grabbed the pencil, held it over the notebook for a second and then began to transform his notes into his latest book.

"One of his earliest memories was lying in the dentist's chair, wanting to be somewhere else, and looking through a large window to find it…"

16

28 July 1990 - Hampton Court

It seemed he had never been away. The bottle of barbiturates was still standing by the whisky bottle on the letter he had received. He allowed the trolley bag to remain by the door. Why unpack it? Now was the day. Now was the hour when he would cease to be. Tommy was distracted by the light on the telephone holster. Curiosity got the better of him. Someone had been leaving messages. He pressed the "play" button.

There were four messages, each of them from Henry Locke, his publisher. There was renewed interest in Tommy's work. Could Tommy ring him back A.S.A.P. By the time Henry left his fourth message, his request was short and to the point.

"Tommy, ring me back as soon as you get this. Thank you."

Tommy dialled. There was a click and Henry's voice crackled down the line.

"Yes... Sorry," Tommy said. "I was in Verona... Yes, uh-huh... Yes... Oh... That's encouraging, yes, that's great, yes… Wait a minute, Henry, you are asking me to write something new… A novella…? Yes, I can write a novella… Inspired by my trip? Yes, indeed but not by Juliet's balcony… Oh, I suppose I just immersed myself in the city and allowed myself to feel its beating heart… Yes, I already have a title… It's because it was you…Yes, it is a love story but I don't have an ending… That's right – no ending… Maybe, but let me work on it. The ending will come… Yes, probably out of the blue… OK, speak soon… Bye.

Renewed interest in his work was something he had not reckoned on. He did not understand it but it must have been growing, unknown to anyone for a considerable period. He wondered when this rekindling of interest had started. And that day would have been followed by countless other days on which interest grew and there was hardly the time to look at it, to measure it before it appeared in his life as a welcome call from his agent. To be invited to write something new – that was truly wonderful. He had scribbled out the first draft while in Verona. OK – he was still searching for an ending but it was only a matter of time.

He stepped towards the bottle of barbiturates, grabbed it by the neck and moved it to one side before doing the same with the whisky bottle.

Somewhere over the palace grounds, a clock struck the hours.

Now for the unpleasant bit, Tommy. Get it over with, man.

He picked up the big and ugly brown envelope and scanned the name and logo above the envelope window: Patton, Boggs, Goodwin and Partners, Solicitors. It seemed they were based in New York. Tommy shook his head and tore at the envelope. There was a cover letter from the company and Tommy skimmed through it. The cover letter concerned the last will and testament of a certain Mrs Patterson, now deceased, of Jacksonville Carolina.

Tommy blinked.

It appeared that the late Mrs Patterson had named him as the recipient of that part of her fortune made during her own distinguished career.

Tommy blinked again.

There must be some mistake.

He had never known anyone by the name of Patterson. He cursed this disturbance. It was a cruel joke - a sort of April fool's prank gone bad.

Mrs Patterson, the letter went on, had married art dealer Rudi Patterson. On Mr Patterson's death, his wealth had passed to his wife but a road accident several months later had led to the demise of Mrs Patterson. The circumstances of the accident were not clear but foul play was not suspected. Police believe that careless driving on the part of Mrs Patterson was the likely cause of the accident. Having no surviving family of her own, Mrs Patterson had left instructions in her will that the money she inherited from her husband be divided among a number of charities. However, the considerable sum of money to which he was now entitled came from the aforementioned proceeds from her personal fortune. Tommy was, therefore, urged to telephone Patton, Boggs, Goodwin and Partners as soon as possible.

Patton, Boggs and Partners had also been instructed to pass on a letter from Mrs Patterson to Mr Mostyn and the epistle was enclosed therein.

Tommy dug inside the envelope and pulled out the smaller personal letter. He opened it and inserted his hand. There were two small objects inside.

He paused for a long, long moment and then pulled out a photo - a man dancing in a sunlit room and smiling at the camera. He turned the photo round in his fingers. Across the back were the words:

"…because it was you…"

He inserted his hand in the envelope once more and pulled out the most fragile Edelweiss and the happiest, the most beautiful memory in the whole wide world.

"One day, one day I will come back to you, Tommy," she had said.

And she had.

Printed in Great Britain
by Amazon

86910809R00072